I0764634

West of the Gospel

WEST OF THE GOSPEL

A Tale of the Fewkes Legacy

W. JOHN MACGREGOR

Published by Gospel Mountain Yarnweavers, an imprint of:

HJ Books
P.O. Box 48282, Burien, WA 98166
http://www.hjbooks.com

Printed in the United States of America

Library of Congress Control Number: 2010922916
ISBN 10: 0-9787554-5-6
ISBN 13: 978-0-9787554-5-4

Cover image © TommyIX. Used by permission.
Cover graphics design by Greg Wright.

For the Heroes of August

Contents

PROLOGUE

Whether the gray of the smoke and ash that had blown the streets of Libby, Montana for the previous five days was darker than the rat's nest atop the head of the crone at Billy Blew's was a tough call. But it didn't matter. The smoke still wandered the deserted streets and hid the morning sun, and Dunn Creek Nell still haunted the worn floorboards and tarnished brass rails at Blew's, though hash—and not whiskey—was now its primary trade.

Back in '92, however, Libby had been a smaller town, and a wilder. Hard rock mining had replaced the placer works on Libby Creek three years earlier, heralding the arrival of the Great Northern line. The glad-handing flow of filthy lucre that habitually accompanied gold and silver mines across the frontier found its way up and down the Kootenai that year. Since Libby Creek, as it was then known, was at the practical edge of the frontier—and the geographical limits of Montana—the easy prosperity brought with it the usual surplus of saloons, claim jumpers, dance hall girls, sure-thing artists, lawlessness and outlaws.

Billy Blew's was a saloon at the head of Mineral Avenue. The Idaho mining strikes of '92 had been bitter, and that summer Blew's place saw the end of one of the strike's uglier aftershocks. Wild Bill "Ash" Montgomery was a local miner and sometime homesteader who, in spite of his reputation, had made a go of both ends of his harsh frontier life. In the good months, he and his wife worked the land on their homestead on the north bank above Kootenai Falls, and proved up in good time, while in the off months he worked for hire in the mines around Eagle City and Murray. It was there, during the early spring of '92, that Wild Bill and his independent streak apparently ran afoul of folks that wanted him dead.

As with the bombing that later killed Idaho's Governor Steunenberg, no one really knew for sure who was responsible for killing Wild Bill's wife: but it has always been assumed it was someone linked to the union; or, more properly, someone linked to an intense dislike for Wild Bill. And so he came to Libby that Wednesday, and to Billy Blew's, looking for trouble and a man named Thomas Fewkes. He found both.

Dunn Creek Nell was at the bar that day in 1892—not working the bar, as you might think; no, even as a young woman Nell was a bit of a crone. She was at a table with her glass and her bottle, and as she looked through the window of Blew's Saloon down the shank of the T from the head of Mineral Avenue, she saw Bill Montgomery coming up the hardpack from the Libby ferry. You could always tell Bill's walk from a distance, with his odd hitching gait.

Dunn Creek Nell wasn't the only one who saw him coming, but she may have been the only one who really saw what happened when Wild Bill Montgomery died. All the county paper would later offer was, "One day he ran into the wrong man with a .44 Smith and Wesson and was removed from things earthly."

On Thursday morning, August 25th, 1910, Blew's was no longer a saloon. In truth, it was no longer even Blew's. The building had been moved when the town was replatted, along with John P. Wall's mercantile building, and so had survived the fire of 1906. But it still fronted

Mineral Avenue, and locals still referred to it as "Blew's"; and Dunn Creek Nell still haunted its worn floorboards and its tarnished brass rails. And so it was that Dunn Creek Nell was the first to see, through the smoke and ash of the Big Blowup of 1910, that Three Card Monte had come to town, walking up Mineral Avenue from the Libby Ferry in search of Blew's—and a man named Thomas Fewkes.

"Damn," she said as she laid down her fork. "Damn if he don't walk like his daddy."

BACKFIRE

There is a difference between willingness
to die for a cause and willingness to kill,
for one only masquerades as true courage.

As with my Colt .44, there was a time when I had use for the truth.

You knew me once, or thought you did. Of course, you now may know me even better. "Three Card Monte" they call me. Now do you know me? This moniker has stuck to me like stink on a minin' camp, but it makes no more sense than most. Much as I disclaim it, the name hangs 'round my neck like a noose. The name precedes me wherever I go, and my reputation travels even faster than the flames this Palouser is pushin' up the St. Joe, screamin' past the gallows on the outskirts of Avery.

If you recognize the lines at the top of this page, perhaps it is because you once thought these words, even believed them. Maybe you once even gave them breath, and so they stuck to me, and I owned them.

1910 has not been a kind year to Avery, nor to me. We were taught, among other things, remember, that the advance of civilization would end the lawlessness of the frontier. If that is so, I am not aware of that happening. Have you been to Taft, or Grand Forks? Probably not. They are as much a local piece of Hell as Eagle City ever was, or was reputed to be. Remember? Whether the mines or the rails, or the timber, too much of a good thing brings out the worst in folk. With the rails came the telegraph, and now the telephone. For me, these have meant not the end of lawlessness, but the fannin' of flames already out of control. It is as if Halley's comet presaged both my own private conflagration, AND the walls of flame that now threaten Avery.

I am writin' you because I am uncertain if the truth about me will ever find you. To be honest, I doubt it. As I sit in chains here through this long, red night, I see only two possible futures. One, the more likely, is that I will die with the rest of the men that remain at Avery, about the time the backfire fails to check the onslaught of the two infernos which are advancin' on the town; and I would not have you believe that I burned twice. It is enough that I shall surely burn once. I dare not hope, however, that these pages will survive what I cannot, and that they will find you even if I can't.

And so I must hope beyond hope for the Second Future (less likely only due to the certainty of the First): that somehow the town will be spared, only to guarantee that I will not. I hope for this future only because then these pages might survive the flames and find you. And so you would not be left with the image of a man worthy of the gibbet.

I am charged with the murder of seven men. I have struggled tryin' to find the words to break this to you, only to be reminded time and again that you have probably heard even worse of me. The handbills claim numbers for me even higher than seven. I personally vouch for neither accountin', but must confess that two men, at least, have died at my hands. Yes, I have killed. But the deaths were an accident, not murder. Like the words of most desperate men, though, my protestations of innocence may chew tough and swallow dry, like hardtack.

So what is my truth? I will remind you that I have already said that it is of no use to me. It is not a tale I have concocted to gain my freedom. No, it is simply my truth, and it is for you, not me.

Two things have always worked against me. The first is my father. You know all about that, and how that can be, even if other folks have always gotten it wrong. The other is my Colt. You may remember that I was always good with a gun. Too good, even, as if I were conceived, some said, defyin' the odds, with saltpeter and iron. The Old Man near took my hide off for the hole I punched in the Sively stovepipe, which somewhat tarnished the pride I felt for hittin' my intended target dead center with my first shot ever. Of course my runty backside was already pretty raw from bein' thrown the other side of the woodpile.

Remember the 4th of July celebrations in Libby? Well, after the Fat Ladies' and Squaw Races were done, I would give Momma the slip and sneak with the older boys over behind Cowell's. The miners would be bettin' their pokes on one fella or the other, but yeah. It seemed like Thomas Fewkes always came out on top. Later, at home, the stories that Momma and Daddy would tell about the shootin' contests would get all legendary, like the tale that was always told about the famous Fewkes Shot in the Sky. But more than once I saw with my own eyes Thomas Fewkes put a bullet in old Lady Liberty, and you did too.

After Momma and Daddy died, that all changed, of course. Before long, I was far and away a better shot than most of the men out back of Cowell's, and dreamed of one day makin' a grand appearance, comin' head to head with Thomas Fewkes in some sort of glorious showdown. And I do mean "show"-down.

I don't think it was news to anyone in Libby, though, that Wild Bill's kid was a crack shot. They all expected me to end as badly as my Daddy did. Funny how, even though they can get things so wrong and twisted, folks end up being right anyway, it seems. But the end has not yet been written, you will remind me.

By the time I came South to Florence, the legend of Wild Bill Montgomery had grown so distorted as to bear no resemblance to the truth. The way the folks around Gospel Mountain told it, Daddy and Thomas Fewkes had run afoul of each other while high-gradin' ore back in '84. They were both in love, the story goes, with the same gal: a pure-as-the-driven-snow saint of a woman, pressed by the health of her aged and lovin' ma to work as a dance hall girl in Eagle City. For over a year the two feudin' miners pursued the girl, she, in the meantime, guardin' her virtue against the would-be suitors with both an iron will and blue steel at need.

On the night the Dance-Hall Girl had decided to accept Wild Bill's proposal, a crazed and drunken Fewkes burst into the Girl's hotel room, guns smokin'. Wild Bill, being down on one knee at the time, escaped the hail of bullets; but the Girl and the kerosene lamp in the corner were not so lucky. In the ensuin' blaze, the Dance Hall Girl died variously of gun-shot wounds or burns, and Wild Bill nearly died himself of burns he suffered tryin' to save the Girl. But his hopes died in the ashes of that Eagle City hotel, and he would spend months recoverin' from his own wounds, vowin' to someday have his revenge on Thomas Fewkes, who had escaped the flames unscathed. I have no doubt that some writer (a good one, maybe, such as Bob Service) will someday make some use of this tale.

And so, the legend continues, years later Wild Bill tracked down Thomas Fewkes to a small border minin' town in Montana. Determined to have his revenge, he declared that he'd burn the town to ash if he had to, but he'd have his day with old Fewkes. So "Ash" Montgomery torched the town as he entered, and, in the smoke and confusion that resulted, killed six men at Blew's Saloon before himself finally bein' gunned down. Now, at least they got the part right about Mister Fewkes coming out unscathed.

But I do know the truth about Momma, and about Daddy. And in some ways the truth is uglier than the legend. But what good would it be to try to tell folks that Daddy, while no self-riser, was no high-grader, neither: an honest minin' man who spent nearly a decade of winters workin' the mines in Wardner; that Momma, while an Eagle City Dance Hall Girl sure enough, was hardly virtuous; that the rivals' fatal quarrel was not over her, but over Unions and the miners' strike in '92; that the fire and hail of bullets in which she died took place that same year, not in Eagle City but on the banks of the Kootenai; that there was plenty of folks doing the shootin', and not just Daddy, at Blew's later the same day; or that Daddy was called "Ash" merely because of the daily dose of wood-ash he consumed in his mush to treat his incontinent bowel?

The lie is a better story, like the colorful ones you might read in Twain, Harte or Service. And so I suffered the lie to persist, while nursin' the truth in my own heart. Hell, the lie was even useful to me: no one dared mess with the bastard kid of Wild Bill Montgomery, himself a gun-totin' menace sworn to avenge his father's death.

Why the Legend of Thomas Fewkes hadn't grown likewise, I don't properly know. First, maybe, because he'd gone to prison, done his time, and been released. I also expect that his Brothers' hangin' put a certain tarnish on their good-natured, fun-lovin' image (you know what I mean). Daddy, by contrast, is dead, and was always cantankerous.

So, in spite of the years I spent ridin' the range down here around Gospel Mountain and Buffalo Hump, I never got close to folks. It was easier to be true to the truth inside myself, lettin' other folks believe their lies, than to try to persuade 'em to see the truth my way. In that way, the truth was still of some use to me. And I was, after all, very good with a gun, and would amuse the local folks with various tricks. The favorite, it seems, is the one where a deck of cards is tossed in the air and I shoot holes in three before they fall to the ground. Savvy? "Three Card" Mont'y.

It is an amusin' trick, I suppose, usually because of the scramble of the kids playin' Fifty-two Pickup while tryin' to account for my three shots. But in practicin' I could never consistently hit four (and certainly never got close to my goal of hittin' on all six shots!).

Rehearsin' pistol tricks, I suppose, is how I first came to the attention of the law. When the rule of Customary Range down here ended, and land got turned over to those Foresty folks, we all knew it meant changes. The easy days of DHS, Kohrs and Grant were over, sure enough. Instead of free range, the government started chargin' the Outfit a fee to run cattle on the land. Worse, timber Cruisers started payin' folks to put in homestead claims, only to sell out later to big timber Companies. Who'd have thought, after the minin' down here played out, that claim jumpers would later start workin' these hills for TREES? So, to keep some semblance of order between the cattle outfits, the timber outfits, the Cruisers, the claim jumpers and the sure-enough homesteaders, the Foresty Department sends out a bunch of COLLEGE BOYS from Yale or some such place. And gives 'em sidearms. How's that?

Naturally, the homesteaders and Cruisers liked to make us cowboys out to be the troublemakers. It wasn't so bad for me, though. Every year or so, they'd send some new greenhorn in to manage affairs around White Bird. Eventually he'd come pokin' around the DHS (that is, I mean, the PCC) corral, or run into me on the Gospel. We'd get to talkin,' and soon enough the college kid would find out I'd read more than Twain and Harte, and names like Darwin, William James and Sigmund Freud would be all through our talk like birdshot through tar paper, if you get my meanin,' and this city-bred college kid would think he'd found himself a pretty fine friend out here in the middle of nowhere. "Sure enough," he'd be thinkin,' "that Tad is a pretty fine fellow."

Then he'd spend time watchin' me, or hear folks tell about my shootin', and he'd start askin' around. Before long, the Ranger would get around to hearin' the yarns about Will Bill and his boy Monte; and he'd start puttin' one club together with four others and comin' up flush. Then I'd start gettin' all legendary in HIS mind, too: a sure-enough book-learned gunslinger with a pedigree. And he'd forget all about the talks we'd had, and how we'd agreed with James' observation that "ye shall know them by their fruits, not by their roots." Soon enough, he'd start keepin' one eye on me whenever I was around. And so the only law we had in those parts, greenhorn College boys who didn't know a shootin' iron from a collar press, would start feelin' pretty nervous about havin' a handy fellow like me so, well, close at hand.

Of course, that was all right by me. I never counted these boys as friends, 'cause I knew they were just as given to buyin' in to legend as most folks (maybe even more so, seein' as they were from Cities and Colleges). And sure enough, about the time he started mistrustin' me, the Service would up and transfer our Ranger boy out to some more meaningful place, and a new one would ship in. And the whole process would start again.

Now, the downside to all of this was the extent to which my legend grew without my knowin' it. When from time to time I'd ride up to Santa or even St. Joe for some entertainment, someone (usually, I must confess, a girl at the Saloon or Dance Hall; I trust you will not judge me too harshly) would tell me about the latest stories which had been told about me in town. It seems that just about every unbelievable gunslinger story told in Idaho in those days eventually got my name attached to it, and usually 'cause some idiot college kid, with a fascination for all things Frontier, would pipe up at the end of some liar's story and say, "Hey, that must have been ol' Three Card that done that! Hell, I used to see ol' Monte do thus and such when I was down on the White Bird..." And there you go. Now these Rangers, and other folks, would be addin' to my legend all over the West, from New Mexico to the Canadian Rockies.

This is how you have come to hear of me, I guess, or my legend. I want to tell you now that whatever you have heard that I have done prior to August of this year (and I know you've heard some), well, it is flat-out false. It's important to me that you believe that. I don't know what all you have heard, but I can see that you might well think me a misguided killer, though you might not judge me. That's just not true. I don't know what else to say.

Well, now. The problems of this August are real enough. But this month's trouble started earlier this spring. I told the Boss that I was figurin' on movin' on after the Spring Drive, when we move the cattle from over East of the Hump down West of the Gospel, from winter range to summer grazin'. This caused quite a stir in the Outfit, since I'd been a hand for goin' on eleven years. Two-Bit Murray, he's the one, you know, who mistook the Old Man's fried grub-worm rheumatiz medicine for bacon grease? Well, Two-Bit comes to me and asks me where I'm headed. "Up to Libby, I suppose," I says, being as economical as possible with my words. When he asks what for, I says, "Got a debt to settle." That's all. And you know I do.

Before sunset it was already all over Florence that Three Card was headed back North to avenge his Daddy's death. Now how do you suppose I am to do that? No matter. Truth happens to an idea, James says. And it looks like in this case he was right.

That was late March. Well, the Business bein' what

it is, and my business not bein' much of its own (so there's not an awful lot to mind most days), one thing happened and another. Soon my plans for headin' up Libby way got way-laid. Long about June, though, I was reminded of my delinquency, if you get my meaning.

Tumbleweeds Tedrick walked into a White Bird hash house in which I spend some time. Now Ted was one of the old-timers from Wardner. He was one of Corbin's men cut loose after the narrow-gauge was pushed through to Wallace and bought out by the Great Northern. Daddy worked with Ted at the Bunker Hill in Wardner from the winters of '87 through '92, so Ted knew the truth about Daddy and figured the truth of me to be about the same.

So Ted sees me at my table in the corner and sits with me. Like the minin' camps he used to haunt, the smellin' of Ted well preceded the seein' of him. But when I saw him, I figured it was him because of the scar that circled his left forearm, mangled when the Sullivan Mine was wrecked durin' the strike of '99. Well, Ted sits and he just looks at me for a good bit, seemin' just to enjoy watchin' me eat. It was good he was enjoyin' it, because my own pleasure was decreasin' rapidly. Finally he spoke.

"Knew yer daddy, kid."

"Yeah. You're Tedrick, aren't you?"

"Oh yeah," he said, takin' a languid look back over his shoulder. He stopped, expectin' me to say something, I think. I was hungry, the grub was good, and I'd paid for it; so I ate.

"Ash was a good friend to me, son. I'd like to think I could be a friend to his kid, too."

"You might be," I said, "but I'm not bettin' the bank on it."

"No, I don't suppose so." He flexed his left hand, habitually, I think. The purple snake on his forearm writhed and shook. "You ain't done the tenth part of what they say you have, have you, son?"

I had a mouthful of hash, and really couldn't offer much of a response other than to blink once or twice. This seemed to satisfy him.

"Yeah, well ain't that a bitch. Now look here, Tad. I just come down through Clarkia, and the Ranger there told me a funny thing."

"Did you laugh?" I asked, seein' that Ted wasn't the jovial type.

"Naw," Ted said, "and I ain't laughin' now, neither."

I joined him in his general lack of mirth. We savored it.

"Look here, Tad," he said, growin' more serious (if that were possible). "You'd best be watchin' your back. You know your daddy and I saw eye to eye on most things."

The irony of this statement was lost on old Ted, who was probably a good foot shorter than Daddy was. I suppressed a smirk, and let the moment pass.

"One of them things was the Unions. Not that Unions are bad in themselves, mind you, but there's a bad element to the Unions around here. I don't need to tell you about the strike of '92."

He didn't. In other parts of the country, organizin' labor had probably been a real good idea, I suppose. But we both can remember the pack-train full of trouble it caused in Idaho, and how it had led not only to Daddy's killin', but the death of several others and injury to scores. Organized lawlessness is still lawlessness.

Ted went on. "And I can see by the way you been watchin' my forearm that you know about '99, too."

Well, I did. I'd come down to the Gospel by then, but I knew well enough.

"Well, look here," Ted says. I looked, always wantin' to be obligin' as possible. And it was a struggle. Ted isn't the best-lookin' of fellas. He scratched his chin just then to prove the point, I guess, and it looked like maybe Santa Claus would come early to White Bird that year.

"Well, look here, " he went on, "I always suspected that it was the strike of '92 that done your daddy in. The Fewkeses were a bad element, spot-on, and I'd seen 'em comin' and goin' at odd hours in Wardner. So it didn't surprise me when I heard that Thomas had done old Ash. The Fewkes brothers sided with the notion that top-side workers like me didn't warrant the same wage rates doin' the riskier work below ground. Now, that's where I'd started out, and I figured I'd done my time, so I didn't see things the same way. And when things got ugly with the Mine Owners' Association, the Fewkes boys had all ended up spendin' time in the Kellogg bullpen that July.

"Now in '99, it seems they'd remembered that I'd cottoned to your daddy's ideas about workin' with scabs in '92, and martial law hadn't learned 'em a thing. So they deliberately hit the Sullivan on my shift. I know this 'cause I saw Thomas there."

Do you know if this is true? This I hadn't heard before. I somehow doubt this to be the case.

Ted didn't, of course. "If he hadn't disappeared, I'm sure they would have brought him up on charges then and there, just like they got Haywood and the others in ought-seven."

Well, Ted got my interest then. I'd followed those trials with great interest, fascinated at the injustice of it all. Imagine, the ex-Governor gets blown to bits at the entrance to his own house (Happy New Year, Mrs. Steunenberg!) over a six-year-old feud, and then it takes TWO YEARS to bring the culprits to Trial! This is progress? It's no wonder that Frontier Justice is still so popular in this day and age: much to my regret and sorrow.

And then they bring in Darrow to defend these men, he arguin' that murder doesn't really matter, but upholdin' the law DOES. "Tomorrow someone else will be murdered," I saw that Darrow had said in the paper, "next week another; and yet the state will go on: the law will be preserved." Tell that to Mrs. S. Lord! There are so many folks that need justice that just don't get it.

Ted continued while my mind burned. "Well, I thought that was that," he says, turnin' his eyes up in his head like he was lookin' for his thoughts somewhere up in his brain pan, tucked under the shameful soft felt hat he wore. "That is, until this here Boy Ranger collars me in Clarkia. 'Lookie here,' says he to me."

Now, I rather doubt the Ranger spoke to Ted that way, 'cause the Rangers weren't "lookie-here" kind of folks like Ted.

"'Lookie here,' says he to me. 'My blue eye's lookin',' says I, 'An' the other one, too.' And this feller tells me that Charlie Dennis, up on the Bull River, heard from Jaydub Redeye that some of Fewkes' old crew near Troy was gettin' a tad restless."

Now, I suppose they might be, at that. And rightfully so. And wouldn't they REALLY be, if they knew what you and I had in mind?

But old Ted, he paused, realizin' that he'd unintentionally used my name as a Part of Speech. This was the kind of thing that supposedly got men new access holes to their innards, and his instincts got the better of his brain in that moment, I think.

"Lookie here," I says, "I don't mind, Ted." My use of his vernacular put him at ease.

"Well, look, son," he continued, "I figure that if the Fewkes crew are gettin' edgy, and some tin-pot law boy in Clarkia can put me and that crew together, I reckon I know the score."

He scratched the stubble on his chin, and the snow on his Mac grew deeper. "They know you're plannin' on comin,' kid, just like ever one else do. So I'll pass on them words from the Clarkia boy to you, son. Best watch your back. I know you're capable."

And so old Tumbleweeds blew out of White Bird down towards Boise, not long after blowin' from this life into the next. Three weeks from that day, I heard he'd had an "accident" back up near Wardner. A lot of folks reckoned it wasn't any such thing.

And a lot of folks think Thomas Fewkes is dead, which may surprise you, just some. Everyone knows Matthew and Steven hung after the job they did with Pine Martin in Conconully, and word was that the third brother had cashed in his chips up in the Okanogan after he'd done his time. Cletus Hanks was known to make the claim, more than once, that he'd plugged Fewkes in a boar's nest during a blizzard up a coulee West of Loomis.

Anyhow, by this time it was mid-July, dead middle of the driest summer in memory. I hear even up on the Kootenai you haven't had a drop of rain since May. Is that true? I imagine you got the same problems up there as we do here. Everywhere there's railroads, with Engines and brakes flingin' sparks on slash and ties on every hillside. Down here, anyway, this has kept our Rangers pretty busy, runnin' on rail Speeders after darn near every train, and organizin' crews of loggers and ranch hands to fight spot fires here and there.

Of course, I've had my share of this kind of work ever since those Rangers came on the scene. Seems that part of the land lease agreement between the Foresty Service and the Outfits is that the Outfits are to supply men at the Service's demand (negotiated as part of the low fee for use of the land). Now, fightin' fires in the first place don't make all that much sense to me; but it sure as heck got to be a serious situation this summer, as, time and again, patches of timber that we "saved" in years past got even drier and went up the minute that some tipsy logger with a smoke even glanced at the trees.

The boys from the Outfit used to look on this fire-fightin' work pretty much as a lark, mostly because the feed was so good, and didn't cost the Outfit a nickel. Even when the hoboes they'd pay out from White Bird to work on the crews would start fires down the line just to keep the work goin' and the grub comin,' the boys would find it all pretty amusin.' But by the first week of August, every time we got called out to give a hand, the boys would start lookin' at each other all funny, you know, like the deacons from the Church do when the Preacher pays a social call to the Barkeep's wife, beggin' your pardon. And some cow puncher with a horseshoe for a brain would have to say, "Oh, this'll be JUST fine about the time a good Palouser kicks up."

It's funny how somethin' that you once just never gave a second thought to can suddenly turn into a life-threatenin' situation.

Now truth be told, until this last week, none of these fires got very big at all, not more than a few dozen acres. This is in part because of the vigilance of these Rangers, and because they suspended timber harvestin' due to the danger. It had also been a long while since there'd been wind anything near as serious as a Palouser.

So, with all the normal Business to attend to, and this spot work with the Fires, I really hadn't had much energy to put into mindin' my backside and all, or makin' preparations to head North.

This brings us to last Wednesday, August 17. Part of our crew had gone down to Slate Creek, to the North and West of the Gospel, to help fight a fire that had flared up at a horse camp on the West bank of the upper Slate. We had worked late into the evenin' diggin' a fire line to the West of the blaze, and then backfired it, expectin' to keep the blaze to the East, confined along the creek bed. It was a low ground fire, settled into the duff and not a crown-popper, and the winds were low so we figured there was little chance of the fire jumpin' to the East bank.

Well, we got back to our camp on the East bank late. I don't really know what time it was, but it was after dark, so about ten o'clock or so. Sometime while we were washin' up was when these three fellas rode into camp, I guess. I didn't see 'em ride in, so maybe they'd been there waitin' for us to return. I don't know.

I'd just headed for the mess line, and noticed this one fella I didn't recognize, sittin' on a horse at my left, holdin' a lantern. Well, I thought that kind of strange, because even though it was dark and we were in need of light, horseback is a strange place from which to provide it. So I'm lookin' this fella in the eye as I walk past, and he's lookin' at me. Just as I look away, puttin' my eyes back ahead of me, towards the cook fire, someone calls out, "Monty!" At this very instant, I also hear the sound of a gun bein' drawn, the sound of steel on gun leather; and it weren't comin' from the fella on horseback. I can't peg the source of that scrape fast enough, but figure someone has seen that I'm about to get shot in the back, and calls out. So I whirl around behind me, spinnin' to the right, continuin' the motion I'd made lookin' away from the rider. At the same time, I draw my Colt while cuttin' my own legs out from under me, knowin' that most folks, if they miss at close range, miss high. Aim for the crotch, and you might hit thc chest or head.

Well, my instincts served me well. A third fella by the fire, who I had neither seen nor heard, fired first. These two shooters figured to catch me in a cross-fire, reducin' the odds of me getting 'em both. Well, the fella by the fire, now behind me, sure enough did miss high, and shot the noisier fella I'd spun to face. Looked like it caught him right in the head. Lyin' on my back, and lookin' upside down toward the fire, I could now see the other, quieter fella silhouetted in the dark, and realized why the rider with the lantern was there. It was so these other two could take pot shots at me in full light.

In self preservation, I figured this fight would be best concluded in the dark, and shot at the lantern. It damn near exploded. I must have hit the tank, because kerosene fire shot in a sheet down that fella's side and all across his rig. The horse, also burnin,' bolted into the woods, rider and all. I quickly gathered my legs under me and faced toward the fire. This fella was now walkin' toward me, firin' wildly as folks scattered. He had no idea where I was. I took my time, and aimed well, takin' him down with a single shot to the shoulder of his gun arm. There was no need to kill him. I suppose there must be some need at times, but this sure wasn't it. So I didn't try. This was the first man I ever shot, and the only one.

Not willin' to take chances on there only bein' three of these guys, I wasn't about to wait for another round of shootin' to start. I reined the first horse I could lay my hands on, and forsook the Gospel, followin' Slate Creek North toward White Bird. This was apparently the route the burnin' horse took, too, because here and there for the first few hundred yards were fresh spot fires sparkin' up in the duff. It seems the fella burned to death, too. That is the other fella I know I killed, and I'm sorry I done it. But it wasn't deliberate.

Now, I'm not terribly slow in the uptake. Nobody had ever tried to kill me before, and the timing weren't coincidence. I wasn't about to head back to camp and settle my affairs before headin' out. I'd had plenty of reason to leave already, and now seemed as good a time as any to actually go: even better than most. I wouldn't need much for the few days' trip up to Libby, and figured I could rely on the boys at the PCC to settle things for the horse and such. I never figured on things goin' sour, from me up and runnin' out like that. It was so obvious that I was bein' jumped, and there were so many witnesses on hand.

But like I said, there was a time when I had use for the truth.

Not long after this, I saw something that should have disturbed me, and I also did something I now regret. On my way out of the Gospel country, I stopped at the Slate Creek Ranger cabin. Porter, the latest Foresty boy, was up on the Slate Creek fire, so the cabin was dark. In my haste to make myself scarce, I mentioned that I'd of course had no time to grab grub, clothing or spare cartridges. So I figured some of Porter's things would do, on real loan, not on cowboy loan.

I found a kerosene lamp quick enough, lit it, and popped up the cabin's rough stairs to rummage through Porter's clothes, findin' a good stout coat and Foresty Service cap. When I came down, I crossed to the desk and left a note for Porter.

This is the thing I regret. "Took some shells for my Colt," I wrote briefly. "You know what for. I'm good for it with the Pacific Cattle Company. Don't need no pay where I'm goin'. Will leave Deeds' roan in Grangeville." Guess Porter had a different idea than I did about what that meant.

As I went to put out the kerosene, I saw it over in corner: the telephone. I didn't make much of it at the time, other than to remark to myself how times were changin'. You know, the West ain't what it was; first the iron horse, and the telegraph. Now electricity, the telephone and horseless carriages. It's the dangedest thing. But, then, you know, the West is still exactly what it was. I lit out.

As it turned out, at that point I should have taken the old pack route that ran from Florence to Mount Idaho. But I had no idea that even an hour would turn out to be a precious loss of time, nor that I would be better stayin' off the beaten track. The wagon road through White Bird to Grangeville was a good road, and a new one, and I thought I'd make good enough time for my purposes. After another stop at Woody's (the hash house in White Bird, you know, where I'd met Tedrick) I made the White Bird ascent at dawn. If ever you get down this way, it's really a sight you should see.

The road comes up out of the Salmon along White Bird Creek, where Chief Joseph's Nez Perce whupped the Army in seventy-seven. There's a small town there, and the road winds like a flaccid snake up the steep ridgeline on the North of the White Bird. The ravines on South of the White Bird gather like folds on the hide of some reclinin' mountain-range-sized elephant. In the spring, the dark green trees shade those folds against the new green of the prairie grass and camas, while the new snow stands out on the peaks of the Gospel and the Buffalo Hump further beyond. Whenever I'm at White Bird, I ride on up the pass to Grangeville just for the sight, even in the brown of August.

The view from White Bird that dawn was dun with smoke, which hid the risin' sun. There would be no pink on the peaks that day. Just orange from the fires now burnin' out on Slate Creek.

From the top of the pass I looked North. If I'd been at sea, I'd have said that the crests of the distant waves were dotted with a score or more ships, steamin' for some distant harbor. But I wasn't at sea, literally. Hopefully, the tell-tale smudges of smoke from August's blazes would be happy where they were, and stay put. It would not be a pleasant road North. I goaded my mount onward.

We covered nearly eighty miles that day, a tough ride without proper boots. I'd had a notion to take a train to the Kootenai. The Camas Prairie line from Grangeville to Lapwai (and then the Northern Pacific to Spokane) would have gotten me to the Great Northern well enough. But the Northern Pacific terminus at Stites was only a few miles north of Grangeville, and the smoke I'd seen at dawn left me unsettled in my mind about tyin' myself to the rails. Many of the fires this summer had been flarin' up along railroad right-of-ways, and the Ranger's gear I'd borrowed from Porter might have required some explainin' to rail crews.

The decision could be put off, I figured, as long as I followed the N.P. line Northward to Orofino. I passed through Kooskia in late mornin', still keepin' to the main road. By the time I got to Pardee that afternoon, I noticed that I was startin' to attract a little more attention than a lone Ranger on horseback ought. Dusk fell as I drew near to Greer, and it was well that I arrived at Orofino under cover of darkness, and that I had stayed clear of the rail lines.

You may not know, but Orofino is as busy and nearly as wild a place as it was in the days that Old Isaac the Walla Walla was still bringin' his cans of nuggets to the Oro Fino bank. Today it's nearly as easy a place to lose yourself, especially after dark. I took Deeds' roan into a copse of Ponderosa up Jim Ford Creek, and made my way into Orofino in my shirt sleeves.

Visits to just three saloons confirmed my suspicions. That telephone in the Slate Creek cabin had done its work, and done it well. The telegraph lines from Riggins to Bonner's Ferry were all carryin' the news that Three Card Monte, a murderous gunslinger, dressed as a Foresty Service Ranger, was headed North, most likely by rail.

Porter, down at Slate Creek, had jumped to some conclusions. He'd rightly guessed that I'd be leavin' the roan at Grangeville because I intended to take the Camas Prairie Line North. But when I told him I'd taken shells, and that he "knew what for," I was mistaken. He didn't have a clue what for.

All Porter knew was that there were two men dead on Slate Creek and another missin', also likely dead. As Porter told the story, I'd fired the first shot and plugged the first dead fella in the head. Now, as I told you, this was the doin' of the man's partner, not mine. Then, says Porter, I'd fired wildly on the rider. As the startled horse bolted, Porter claimed, I set my sights on the third man, merely wingin' him. (I now know that he later died from loss of blood in the ensuin' confusion, after professin' ignorance about why I should have opened fire unprovoked. So, I guess I sure enough did kill this fella, too.)

Worse, Porter claimed that I deliberately set fire to the Nez Perce Forest on Slate Creek to cover my escape, and then stole his Ranger's gear as a disguise. I was to be considered armed and extremely dangerous, a tough proposition in a country with little law but scattered Sheriffs and a few Foresty boys. The word was out that I was headed for the Kootenai and revenge, and the rail lines were notified to be on the lookout.

The Forest Telephone lines from Slate Creek to Pierce and the other Ranger cabins required only one connection to the web of telegraph lines crisscrossin' the rail network in Idaho. Porter's message had gone before me.

I passed a sleepless night back on the Jim Ford as I debated what to do. It wouldn't be my last.

You might well ask what I debated. You could point out that if I had done nothin' wrong, I had nothin' to fear. You could remind me that a man on the run indicts himself with his feet. You could also ask why I didn't just discard Porter's coat and hat, and come directly to you.

I can only tell you that, in my mind, I had not only been indicted, I had already been tried and found guilty. Often enough over the years, I'd seen lynch mobs do their work: efficiently, ruthlessly and often with great inaccuracy. The risk of livin' on the run seemed less to me than trustin' the better, more civilized nature of my fellow men. Ha.

There are many roads that leave the Gospel, but they all lead to the Kootenai well enough. Comin' through

Orofino, I could easily avoid rail lines to Clarkia if I wanted, except for the final fifteen miles or so. And from there, the road North could be pretty isolated, with only the need to jump the new tracks below Avery, the old ones at Wallace, and a couple other spots. The lines would cross my path, though, for the most part, and not run parallel, as they would if I traveled up through Coeur d'Alene and the Pend Oreille.

Besides, I had no plans to return to the Gospel. I'd been ready to make my break most of the summer, and now was on my way. I hadn't let you know, sure. But there was now no goin' back for me. So I really couldn't see any sense in givin' myself up.

Now, the coat and hat: that's a prickly pear, sure enough. I guess it seemed so natural to pack a coat and hat that it just didn't occur to me to leave 'em off. But that led to another odd predicament, one that I'll tell you about right quick.

So before first light, the roan and I were off again. My strategy the second day was a little different. Whenever a large party would approach (I was still travelin' fast enough to cover roughly sixty miles that day, and was not overtaken, but once) I would guide the roan off the beaten path and rejoin the main road after the party had passed. In this way I expected to avoid any armed confrontation, as smaller groups and solitary travelers would hardly be likely to challenge me even if I were recognized.

Durin' the early part of the day, I hit some hot spots near Dent, some flare-ups. They were scattered, and had been controlled by fire crews well enough to keep 'em isolated. But they pretty well blocked my path of progress, and I didn't care to get anywhere too close to a fire fight. Crews had been clearin' fire breaks for several days, it appeared. So it seemed best at that point to leave the trail for Clarkia, avoidin' the W. I. & M. line below Jersey on

Elk Creek altogether. Instead, I set out for the trails up the Clearwater North Fork. From there, I figured, I would have my choice of paths into St. Joe country, as I'd already planned, or strike Easterly via the Old Montana Trail on the Little North Fork into Deborgia.

So it came about that probably the worst thing possible happened. Just after I'd struck the Little North Fork, long about dusk, a rider comes up hard behind me. I'd just passed a bend in the trail, and I was restin' the roan, leadin' her on foot, so I didn't hear the rider until it was too late. In the gatherin' darkness, the rider mistook me for someone else, and started hollerin', "Halm! Joe Halm!" When I stopped to face the rider, it became apparent that he was greatly surprised to find that I was not Joe Halm, nor any Ranger he recognized. He reined in his mount, stared at me open-mouthed for a short moment, then turned and bolted off the way he came.

I later found out that Halm was a Ranger leadin' a crew on the upper St. Joe and Clearwater drainages, and that the rider had been sent to warn him to be on the lookout for a road agent called Three Card Monte. When he encountered me, he apparently judged his message superfluous, havin' done the lookin' out himself, and high-tailed it for Elk River. From there the word went out that I was headed into the Clearwater and St. Joe country, the telegraphs clickin' and telephones ringin'.

Of course, I had no idea of that at the time. By the smell in the air, though, and by the early-gatherin' darkness, I could tell that I was gettin' close to other burns. I decided to settle in for the night and get some much needed sleep. I had not slept since the night of the 16th; it was now the night of the 19th. I staked the roan in a small meadow and waited until daylight to get a better look at the lay of the country. If I'd only known what the morning of the 20th would bring, I would have pressed on into the night (though perhaps the only safe trail for me would have been back toward the Gospel).

I woke well past first light, in spite of my vigilant intent. The air was murky and close, and though the sun was well up it was just a dull red ball, its rays obscured by smoke. I couldn't tell for sure, but I guessed that there were a number of fires burnin' in the Clearwater. I hastily rolled up my bed and got on the way.

Now the extent of yearly burnin' in the Selway and Clearwater basins (and the reasons those fires have historically originated) is hotly debated by Foresty boys. But the fact is that the country changes when you pass from the Clearwater into the St. Joe. The Clearwater is heavy with Ponderosa, mixed with stands of old Cedar, and at higher elevations the Lodgepole. But the St. Joe is a mass of White Pine. It's a funny thing, but when you read Bret Harte or even Bob Service, you get the impression that the whole of the West has been tamed and settled for decades. But until the silver panic in ninety-three, river pigs, timber cruisers and claim jumpers were unknown in the St. Joe. Hell, the Indians themselves didn't do much more than cross the upper valley from time to time, and Ferrell (that is, St. Joe itself) wasn't even platted much before ten years ago. But the failure of the mines, never plentiful in the St. Joe basin (and the Idaho Legislature's funding of new roads) opened up an entirely new use for the St. Joe. Until pretty recently, it was as unsettled and wild a place as you could ever find in the West.

But when those stands of giant White Pine were discovered, things began to change. I've heard lumbermen claim that there's some fifteen billion board feet of lumber in the St. Joe drainage. How much is a billion, anyhow? That's enough trees to keep six thousand men busy for fifty years, they say. By ninety-eight, they were takin' out sixty-five million board feet, and I heard that last year the total ran up to nearly half a billion, thanks to the Milwaukee and St. Paul line over to Taft they just completed last year.

You remember hearin' about the wild days of Eagle City? You might not believe what goes on in Taft and Grand Forks, and I wouldn't want you to see it. These little hellholes are undoubtedly the most ungodly towns this side of Chicago, rivalin' any legends of what folks are already callin' the Old West. You might not know this, but at the summit of the Bitterroots, they punched a two-mile tunnel through the top of the mountain. At the East end is Taft, and on this side is Grand Forks. These burgs sprang up to take the construction crews' money, and there's no end of liquor, whores and gambling. Honest to God, the men are so drunk and played out it's wrought havoc in the St. Joe valley. It used to be that timber crews were the greatest fire danger in those parts, but I was in Grand Forks last year when the Foresty boys had to come in there and shut down the saloons! Drunk railroad crews startin' forest fires. Imagine that! I bet that's somethin' they didn't teach those boys at Yale.

It's a good thing they've got some men like Ed Pulaski with 'em. You might remember hearin' about him bein' from Wardner. I met him in Grand Forks. Impressive lookin' fella. Lean and tall, better than six foot it looked like. A good steady eye.

I had no idea what was happenin' in the St. Joe this year, but I figured it had to be better than what appeared to be shapin' up to the East in the Clearwater. I was wrong, of course. So I struck North toward the main track of the Old Montana Trail, hittin' it near the trail's peak above the Little North Fork, to its West. That was about noon.

And that's when things started to get out of control. From the switchback, I could see that a big fire was burnin' out to the East. But the smoke was so heavy, I couldn't tell if it was in the upper St. Joe, where the trail would take me, or in the Clearwater a little to the South.

Worse, I could hear a continuous low muffled roar, something like a distant rumblin' of thunder. Ashes, burned leaves and needles began to fall like heavy snow. Where I was at on the East slope of the rise, there didn't seem to be much wind at all, but I rightly guessed that there were severe winds higher up, and that there was fire to the West, as well as to the East. It looked like a Palouser was kickin' up, hot wind blowin' up from the Columbia basin, on over the Palouse and right through the St. Joe to the top of the Bitterroots. And I was right in its path.

The winds were undoubtedly goin' to kick up a pretty fierce firestorm. As I saw it, I had two choices. I could strike East on the Trail, leavin' me some forty miles of rough trail to the summit; or I could backtrack West a bit, and take the fork North to Avery, about twenty-five miles. I didn't like the idea of backtrackin' into a fire, but it seemed wise to try to flank the fire rather than outrun it to the East.

As I crested the rise back toward Clarkia, the full force of the wind hit. And I do mean hit. Deeds' roan stumbled, and darn near turned and ran, but I spurred her down into the Marble Creek junction at a gallop. I'd made the right choice, sure: there was no way I going outrun that fire to the East. But I was still going to have the ride of my life if I was going to flank that fire to the North. I dug my heels in and rode hell-bent for leather.

The roar of the wind rose and live embers began to fall. Somewhere, there was a horrific crown fire bein' chased like the devil by that wind. Before long, the sound of the conflagration was like a distinct roar, like a great number of locomotives going every which way. I almost believed that I could feel a vibration in the earth, stronger even than the poundin' of the roan's hooves. The ashes and embers became thicker and a few pieces of bark and burned twigs began to shower around.

The trail to Avery, after leavin' the Marble Creek

junction, heads down into the headwaters of the Little North Fork of the Clearwater. I hoped to find some sheltered spot there in the creek bed, and as I rushed down the slope I saw that I wasn't alone. The gray pall was changin' minute by minute, and darkness seemed not far in the offing, but I could see that these men I was comin' up on were soldiers: four of 'em. Colored men they were, which surprised me. There were plenty of Chinese down around the Gospel, and had been as long as there had been minin' camps. But I'd never seen much of black men, and certainly never in uniform.

They were in the creek bed, confusedly attemptin' to control their horses, who were naturally spooked. There wasn't any time for small talk or introductions. They were grateful to have someone on hand who seemed to know what to do in a fire, and they quickly followed my directions. A short ways above the place where the trail crosses the Little North, a large rock about thirty feet high abuts the stream, and overhangs it slightly. We blindered the horses and led 'em upstream. I expected that if things didn't get too bad, we could shelter below the rock in the stream bed and wait for the worst to blow over. We unsaddled the horses, wet down their blankets and spread 'em over head and back. The soldiers had their own gear, and I instructed 'em to do the same for themselves.

By now, burnin' embers sailed over us like shootin' stars. It was dark, but still only mid-afternoon. It was hard to tell exactly what time it was. Small fires were startin', in the duff and dry branches, from the live embers rainin' down, and flames sprang up all around. The White Pine of the St. Joe were going to be in trouble this year.

Above us, the air was full of flyin' pieces of burnin' wood, limbs and bark. The horses weren't goin' to make it through this, I saw. As I doused my coat and hat in the stream and threw 'em over me, I yelled to the soldier nearest me, "I've got to get the horses out of here. They won't survive this!" He looked at me strangely, and though I could not hear all his words I could tell that he said, "You're Three Card, ain't you? We were sent to arrest you."

I grabbed him roughly by the upper arm and spoke directly and forcefully into his ear. "Look," I said, "just do what I tell you and you'll make it through this. Lie down in the stream bed, and keep wettin' your blankets down to cover your backs and heads. Breathe through the wet blanket, and don't try to get up, run, or come up for air. The water is going to get warm, and you may soon start to see dead fish. But don't worry: ash in the water is what kills 'em, not just heat. These cedars along the creek bed may even catch fire, but if you stay put, keep wet and keep your heads down you should live to see another day."

"What are you going to do?" he asked. I didn't stop to answer. I didn't really know for sure if those buffalo soldiers were goin' to make it through this, but I was pretty sure that I wouldn't want to come out the other side with 'em, and all of us alive together. That was sure death for me, too. I was takin' the risky route, that's for sure.

I untethered and unblindered the horses, unsure which was which, and as I turned 'em loose they joined the parade of other animals fleein' the fire. As I got to the last horse, I looked back and saw a good-sized black bear join the soldiers wallowin' in the pool beneath that rock.

In desperation, and not knowin' what else to do, I literally took the tail of the last horse as it bolted North on the trail toward Avery. It may seem too strange to be true, but somehow I kept pace with and a hold of that horse as it raced the next few miles. That portion of the trail was uphill, comin' up to the divide between the Clearwater and the St. Joe, so I suppose the horse just mostly pulled and dragged me uphill. Still, I could hear huge White Pine begin crashin' down in the forest around us: not burned yet, but crushed by the onslaught of the hot wind, which had been whipped up into a ferocious and scaldin' gale by the Palouser and the suction of the racin' crown fire. The horse, I'm quite sure, dragged me over more than one of those snags. But I honestly don't recall. Men survive keel-haulin', I hear, and this couldn't have been much different. I was heat-blind, hoof-whupped, torn and ragged, yet still miraculously free of burns.

After some miles, I don't rightly know how many, we did flank that fire. The horse slowed its pace, but I did not lose my grip on its tail. I still could not see, maybe for heat blindness, maybe for darkness, or both. The heat and the smoke made it hard for me know exactly where we were, or which direction we were headed. The horse, though, knew how to find trail, and acted like it knew this one in particular. This was probably because it had been over the trail just a few hours before. I had taken one of the soldiers' horses in the confusion. What happened to Deeds' roan, I have no idea.

After a couple hours headin' downhill from what had apparently been the crest of the divide, we came to the St. Joe. Both up and down stream, in the darkness, I could hear voices on the water as the soldiers' horse and I slaked our thirst. We crossed to the rail right-of-way on the North side, and there by the tracks a little bulldog pup shivered and whined. It was not cold at all, but the pup was terrified: left behind, it seems, by somebody in a panic. You'd have liked that pup. I stuffed her inside my coat and slung myself bareback onto the horse, lookin' in horror as the entire St. Joe valley to the West glowed orange with fire: as far down as St. Marie's, it looked like. There was fire behind me, and fire below me. Not knowin' what else to do, and exhausted, I let the horse take me into Avery, five miles up the track, to the East.

Before long, it became clear that I was not alone in seekin' refuge in Avery. And this was good news, for me. Just after passin' a family who'd loaded their entire cabin into an ox-cart, I came upon the strangest thing. Through the gloom, I could see, on the slope above the rail line, a mine adit with block and tackle strung before it. At one end of the rope was a rather prosperous lookin' man. At the other was a piano, strung up cockeyed like an elk in camp. My curiosity got the better of me, so I rode up to offer my help. From the way I was lookin' at that fella, he could tell I was somewhat amused. Holdin' to the rope and sweatin' like he'd already been through the fire, he paused and looked me in the eye. "You may not be able to take it with you," says he, "but every dern thing can be put in a hole in the ground."

I found the humor to laugh and the strength to help with the rope. It did occur to me, as I worked on the business end of that tether, that I might soon enough be at the opposite end of one those myself. Everything can be put in a hole in the ground. Yessir.

This fella was sure concerned with his piano. It never occurred to him to ask where I'd been, or where I was goin'. But he proved conversant enough about what was happenin' with the fires. Since I'd been on the move for three days, I was glad for the news, if not particularly happy about what I heard.

Seems the whole Idaho panhandle was ablaze. About the time I had been cuttin' fire line down on Slate Creek, Ranger Debbitt in Avery had called in the reinforcements to fight the fires in his area. The Governor sent in buffalo soldiers, Company G of the 25th Infantry. Other Letters of the Alphabet were fightin' fires in Wallace and over the line in Montana. The big work before today had been on a burn East of Avery which had been threatenin' to take out the rail line: started, no doubt, by embers from a steam engine. But the winds which had caught me at the Little North Fork that afternoon had likewise been kickin' up the whole length of Idaho, and things were now thoroughly out of control. The worst of it so far, it seems, had been up at the top of the Milwaukee and St. Paul line.

The fires up and down the St. Joe were gettin' the best of firefighters, trained and untrained, and all of 'em, it seems, had joined a trail of settlers and miners high-tailin' it for the relative safety of Avery. It's a rail town gathered to the shores of the St. Joe River and bunched around the tracks and roundhouse of the Milwaukee and St. Paul.

The first casualty had apparently been Grand Forks, up at the near side of the St. Paul tunnel. As I mentioned before, it's a ram-shackle wild place (or was, I should say). Most of the residents, rail workers, were away from town when the fire hit, of course: away or drunk. The rest, hangers-on like saloon-hall girls, bartenders, sure-thing artists, faro dealers and the like, grabbed what they could (mostly green, gold and silver) and tried to keep ahead of the fire by racin' down the tracks to Falcon, a mile away. When Falcon telegraphed Kyle, a little further down, sayin' that their own little burg seemed doomed, a work engine was sent up from Avery to evacuate the town. Already the trestles between Avery and Falcon were burnin'. But the Engineer, a man named MacKeddin, managed to get that train to Falcon just in time, pickin' up the folks there as the town burned to the ground. By the time he got her back to Kyle, that burg was burnin' too. With the train full, and men hangin' from the boxcars, runnin' boards and cowcatcher, MacKeddin slowly pushed the overloaded engine over the burnin' trestle below Kyle, and picked up the section crew at Stetson before returnin' to Avery to a hero's welcome. It was good that it was a downhill grade.

Out of the bacon grease and into the pitch-wood, as they say. By the time I got into Avery last night, every town to the East, from Grand Forks down to Avery, had either been burned or evacuated. And fires were still comin' up from the West. Where were we to go?

Taft, on the other side of the divide at the opposite end of the St. Paul, East of the Bitterroot divide, had burned as well. Before the telegraph lines to the outside world went down, word had it that the tunnel itself was a haven for hundreds of refugees, and that even Deborgia (you know, over in Montana on the Clark Fork) was burnin'. Down river on this side, the St. Marie's valley was bein' evacuated by barge and rail where possible. But the fire was between us and St. Marie's, and comin' our way. A few brave desperate souls, those voices I'd heard in the gloom down river, had taken to the shoals of the shallow St. Joe, tryin' to float themselves past the fires. I hope to God they gave it up when they saw the wall of flames leapin' the river below 'em. This ain't no typical summer blaze. Not by a long shot.

Debbitt called in the buffalo soldiers and put 'em to work keepin' peace in Avery. There were probably two to three times the normal number of people in town by yesterday, and all of 'em desperate: and many wild to protect the riches they carried with 'em. When all your worldly possessions are in your pockets, you can get mighty nervous.

My own pockets were dang near empty. My stomach was emptier; but I'd found a few greenbacks in Porter's coat, so I figured I'd still be able to get some grub in Avery, though the price would no doubt be high. The smart money would be with those wise folks who always follow desperate men to line camps, boom towns and cattle depots. A place like Avery on a night like this, I knew, would have its own share of men (and women) eager to turn a buck. In the chaos, I figured, I could easily blend in.

And I was too right. Maybe it was too easy to blend in. As I came into town, close on to nine o'clock, the bulk of the 25th Infantry was preoccupied with the rollin' stock at the West end of Avery. On a large flat alongside the St. Joe, the Milwaukee line had constructed a huge oval roundhouse and depot for fuelin', waterin' and servicin' their cars and engines. From up and down the line, they had been sendin' the rollin' stock into Avery for safety, and the buffalo soldiers were there tryin' to organize and guard it all. There was some legitimate concern, I reckon, about citizens tryin' to take trains and make a crazed run for safety somewhere, and the Company wasn't havin' none of that.

The town itself was burstin' to the seams. A makeshift kitchen had been set up at the School House along the boardwalk above the tracks in town. But I wasn't too interested in arm-and-a-leg soup, nor in seemin' too much like a refugee. So I walked the Army pony into town and tethered her in front of the Avery Hotel and General Store, then backtracked to the Restaurant close on up the street.

If I'd had any food with me at all, I sure enough would've skipped payin' for a meal last night. The steak and eggs they served took my last ten dollars, and they even made me pay up front; but I can guarantee you I savored every last bite.

I was sure enough right about what I'd expected to see in Avery, and it wasn't just the prices for food. The talk was wild and varied in the Restaurant last night. Tables were crowded and boisterous, and there wasn't any such thing as a private booth. Folks would come and go, most in a rush, and plop themselves down anywhere there was an open seat.

After I'd got through about five-dollars worth of my steak, the fella beside me got done boltin' his food, and I was joined by an oddly jocular hombre. He seemed pleased as punch about what was goin' on, and proved mighty talkative. He was a wiry, dark fella of average size: a reporter for a paper in Seattle, over in Washington.

So you spent some time there durin' the rush days in ninety-eight? Or was that after? I wish I could have seen that once. I know what gold frenzy looks like in a place like Elk City; but I'd dearly love to see what it looks like when an honest-to-God city like San Francisco or Seattle gets the grip. Was it that winter when Seattle took five feet of snow, or was it the next? The reporter says that was forty-eight inches, and it was '80. Guess I was off by a bit.

Anyhow, this reporter has been a good friend to me. You'd like him, I think, and a man can use a good friend when he's waitin' to have his neck stretched: but I'm gettin' ahead of myself.

He sits down at my table, like I said, throwin' down a rolled leather map case in front of him. He's as pleased as punch, it seems, just to be in Avery and sittin' in this two-bit-gone-four-and-a-half-overnight chow scow. Now, he may have been scared half witless, sure, but he was dern pleased nonetheless. And he gives me this eager look like he's just waitin' for me to ask about that map case. So I oblige.

"What you got there?" I ask around a mouthful of tough rib-eye.

"My notes," says he.

"You a musician?"

He laughed, pushin' back the hard-boiled hat on his head. You can tell a lot about a man by the kind of hat he keeps. A derby ain't a workin' hat, you know, if you know what I mean. "I'm a reporter," he says. "Hod Geiss. I freelance for the paper in Seattle."

He'd been sent out by the Seattle Times to cover the Idaho fires, and as far as he was concerned, he was coverin' what was shapin' up to be the Story of the Century thus far. He was a whistle punk in his element, you know: like a blue-bottle roostin' on a cow chip. Young, fresh, excitable.

I looked at his hands as he picked up his map case and ordered "what he's having" from the biscuit slinger, a young gal who looked like she'd been pressed into service from the kitchen. I don't think she spoke much English.

"You ain't been in that line of work long, I reckon: writin' I mean," I says, indicatin' the reporter's hands.

"Long enough," Geiss says. "I'm a court reporter, mostly. On the side (the broad side, these days) I do carpentry for an old boss of mine by the name of Benton. He was a lawyer once, but now he builds houses. He came out from back East, like me."

That accounted for the rough look of his hands. He loosed the thong on the map case, and out came a sheaf of papers. He pulled a stubby carpenter's pencil from a pocket in his buttoned vest.

"Notes," I observed.

He made an affirmative verbal response that somewhat resembled "Yep" but took about three syllables to do the same work. His jaw was workin' extra hours without gettin' paid for it.

"I got a contract from the Times to cover this flare-up. I managed to get into Avery on the last train through from down St. Marie's way this morning."

"Freelance: what's that?" I inquired.

He made that sound again. "I just pick up the work when I can get it," he says. "It's not my regular job." He started in makin' more notes on his papers.

"You say you ain't from around these parts?" Not that I'd needed to ask, nor that he'd needed to tell me.

"No. I was raised in Hartford, Connecticut." His jacket seemed to be bindin' him, and it was plenty warm that night.

"Mark Twain's town."

"Yes, that's right." He seemed surprised that I'd know. Now, Hartford's probably more famous for its Colt factory, but that's not a conversation I particularly wanted to have with a reporter.

"You ever meet Mr. Clemens?" I asked, genuinely interested.

"Why, yes, once. But I never spoke with him."

"That's too bad," I says, disappointed.

"It was ought-five, I think," Geiss continued. "I'd gone to New York, and had been invited by a friend to the Players' Club. I gravitated toward a table where another novelist, Booth Tarkington, was waxin' eloquent under liquid encouragement, and Twain was with his party."

"Tarkington," I says.

And we both say at almost the same time, "*The Conquest of Canaan.*"

We laughed. "Dang fine book," I says. Geiss was beginnin' to take a shine to me.

"How do you come to read Tarkington?" Geiss asked.

"I don't follow." My last five dollars was gettin' cold on my plate, so I went back at it.

"Well, I mean Tarkington's a Princeton man, an Indiana state legislator. You look…" And here he paused to give me a good lookin' over, and for the first time he noticed the dog's wee curled tail stickin' out of my jacket. I'd given the she-pup a few bites of steak early on, and it had settled in to sleep before Geiss sat down with me.

"You look like you've been fighting fires, or I've never seen shmirkez on a bagel. But I'd say you were a cowhand more than anything."

Well, this caught me a bit. "How do you figure that?" I asked.

"In the first place," he says, "you tend to want to straddle a chair, rather than sit in it proper."

I shifted a bit at this, as it made me feel somewhat conspicuous.

"The other thing is your jeans. They're a good deal messed up from the work you've been doing."

Well, he was right enough about that. He was sittin' to my right, not across from me, and could see my clothes well enough.

"But that don't stop me," he goes on, "from seeing that you ordinarily wear chaps. It's the wear patterns around your hips and the backs of the legs."

And then he smiled real big. "And of course, the Colt's a dead give away. You wear it like a cowboy. Frontier model, isn't it?"

I hadn't wanted to go there. "Peacemaker .44, yeah."

"Same frame as the original '73 model, rechambered for the standard Winchester .44 cartridge." He was from Hartford, sure. "And I just don't figure a cowhand (nor a fire fighter) has got an awful lot of use for Tarkington."

"I got a soft spot for dogs," I explained with a wink. "And Tark does, too."

He spouted some more useless syllables and laughed again, takin' down some notes that looked like chicken scratchin's to me.

He noticed I was lookin'. "Stenographer's shorthand," he says, "picked it up from court reporting. 'You'll thank me someday, Hod,' said Benton. He was right." He looked up at me and took a deep breath. "Now, where have you..."

I had an idea where he was headed with his question, wantin' to know too much about where I'd been and such, so I interrupted. "Hod: Your daddy a coal miner?"

The reporter chortled. "Not hardly. He's a baker. My folks came over from Odessa, and I was born during the voyage over. They carried me off the boat in a coal scuttle, and the name for that precious object was one of the first English words they learned." He grinned a crooked smile. "I've paid the price for that knowledge all my life."

It was my turn to laugh. "That's a good one," I says. His steak came, and I took the opportunity to press him for details about what he knew about the situation with the fires. I didn't figure I needed to know much more, but it would get his mind off questionin' me, I reckoned. Between bites, he started to fill me in on what was goin' on in town, referrin' to his notes for some of the details.

The telegraph and telephone lines were still up a ways down the valley, he said, but communication with the outside was completely down. So he wasn't goin' anywhere for the time bein', not able to file a story until he could either get the story out via telegraph, or get out himself. And he didn't seem too much in a hurry to do the latter. He was enjoyin' himself.

Odds makers, he said, were hourly changin' the line on whether and when fire would take Avery. Lowest odds was now on "yes," and "dawn tomorrow." Bettors figured, I guess, that they might lose everything they had. But if they did, they could still make some profit on the exchange by guessin' correctly when they'd lose their own shirts.

Others were figurin' on coverin' themselves two ways, by bettin' AND by buyin' insurance. There was a run on insurance, in fact. Lines were longer at makeshift brokers doin' business in the canvas shack next door than at the town's company bank—and the longer things went, the higher the insurance rates generally went.

At another table, a conversation was runnin' somethin' very strange. Because the winds had died down after what normally would have been dusk (a few hours before this) some of the more optimistic folks were speculatin' that the fires might die down altogether. A wind, they said, always kicks up at the leadin' edge of a weather front: so rain was sure to follow, especially now that the winds had died. Lower winds and a steady rain would sure enough kill these fires, they reasoned, so another opportunity presented itself.

These folks at this other table had worked up a scheme to sell futures on fire insurance rates, or some such thing. The only kind of stock in my portfolio is a steer, so I don't rightly know how such a thing works. That reporter, Geiss, is still tryin' to explain it me, but I just don't understand. All I can gather is that those men thought there was some way of makin' money if skyrocketin' insurance rates crashed but the fires still materialized. I think they were basically dreamin' of sellin' insurance to the insurers.

At long last, well after his own steak had gotten to the point of no longer seein' daylight, Geiss got around to askin' me some questions. I was naturally skittish about sayin' much, so I begged his pardon and began to rise. But he put out his hand and stayed me with but light pressure on the forearm of my jacket.

"Don't go," he says. "I want to know more about what's been happening on the fire lines."

"You've a better chance, you know, of findin' offal out the back door of a butcher's than at a Chinee laundry, Hod," I says. "The folks up at the District Office can tell you plenty, I reckon." The North Fork Ranger's cabin, I knew, was somewhere here in Avery.

He nodded and muttered some more. The bulldog pup sneezed inside my jacket. "But they're awfully busy," Geiss says. "You've obviously got some time to spare."

"Huh," says I.

He lifted his hat and ran his hand through his dark hair. He seemed to have an instinct for runnin' his pencil stub down the part at the crown of his head. "Where have you been working?"

I looked at him hard as he pulled his derby down to his ear tops again. "Slate Creek," I says, not tryin' to be cagey or anything', just closed-mouthed.

Geiss raised an eyebrow. "I hadn't heard the fire was that close yet."

"Close?" I says.

"Five miles? That's pretty close."

I didn't correct him, but I didn't agree with him, either. If he wanted to take what I'd said wrong, that was his business. On my end, I took his question to mean that there was another Slate Creek in an area nearby. (It's just five miles below Avery, I later learned, very near where I first struck the St. Joe.) "Well, that was back on the 17th," I says, "and it was but a small fire. Typical summer blaze."

"The 17th, huh?" He scrunched his face together. "But you look like you've seen action more recently than that."

I looked down at myself. I was sure enough a sorry sight.

"I reckon," I says. "But I sure enough ain't seen a bath nor barber since the 17th."

By the look on the reporter's face, I could tell he believed the truth of that. He was a well-scrubbed dude with a coat, vest and boiled collar, and if he'd found my odor pungent I could that tell he hadn't spent much time around men the likes of Tumbleweeds Tedrick.

"From Slate Creek," I says, wantin' to turn aside the horns of this conversation, "I went up into the Clearwater country."

"Wait just a minute," the pencil-jockey says, makin' more notes. "Were there any men hurt on Slate Creek?"

"Charcoal punchers?" I says, now bein' a little cagey. This evoked a few more strange syllables from Geiss. "Nah," I says, truthfully. "It was but a simple duff fire. Some folks," I hastened to add, "might've been hurt after I left. I don't know."

Geiss nodded. "All right. But the Clearwater: Ranger Halm was sent in there, wasn't he?"

"Joe Halm?" I asked, recognizin' the name from the leather-slappin' rider I'd met on the trail East of Elk River two days before.

"That's right," says Geiss, feelin' like he was on to somethin'. "You were with Halm's crew? I didn't think they'd been heard from."

"Well, we were separated," I offered, not goin' into

detail about how much distance separated us (since I didn't rightly know, though I could guess some), nor makin' clear that we'd never been together to start with. Those were my details, not the reporter's, I figured. To keep him from breathin' too close, I went on. "In fire county, Pulaski once told me…"

"Ed Pulaski?" Geiss scribbled.

"Yep. He once told me…"

Geiss interrupted me again. He'd apparently learned something about the personalities of the area, and was quite taken with the former plumber and sometime grub-staker. "You know Ranger Pulaski?"

"Well," I says, stretchin' only my back and not the truth, "I worked a fire with him once. Don't properly reckon you could say I know him." The pup began to stir. "But he told me that in fire country, you don't have to look too far to find a blaze with your name on it. I found my own, yesterday, sure enough. I was with a small group of men on the Upper North Fork when the fires hit."

This distracted Geiss sufficiently. It was exactly the kind of story he wanted to hear. I offered him the tale of my flight from the Little North, omittin' details about the color of those men's skin, and about their employer. He also got the impression, it turned out, that those four men had come out with me.

"Do you know where those men from your crew are? I'd like to talk with them," says Geiss. He started to get his things together.

"Well," I speculated, soundin' more confident than I actually was, and wavin' vaguely off to the South, "they're down along the river. We got kind of thrown in together, though, so I don't rightly know their names or nothin'." I didn't bother to mention which river it was I reckoned they were along. I also refrained from speculatin' about the status of their health.

"Well, that's okay," says Geiss. "I'll ask around."

I rose to leave, and Geiss stood with me, leavin' his papers be for a moment. He offered me his hand and looked up at me with a clear gray eye. There was thrill in it, but there was also terror.

I took his hand. "I reckon you're scared, ain't you?" He didn't respond, just looked at me steadily. He had a carpenter's hand, sure enough. Strong but gentle. "You should be. I am, too."

He turned back to his papers. "Take care of that pup," he says. And laughin', he looked back at me and added, "'Not the empty gloves, Joe. Not the gloves.'" A quote from Tarkington's *Conquest of Canaan.* I hope you've read it. If you haven't… do. You'll understand.

When I left Geiss at the restaurant about midnight, he'd gotten the distinct impression that I was a Foresty Service man who'd been workin' the fire down Slate Creek way West of Avery, and had been sent in to help with the work in the Clearwater. Halm's name had been mentioned, and Pulaski, and these were names he knew. I could see his mind was chewin' on what had been left unsaid, though, and the price of that chewin' turned out to be far greater than what he and I'd paid for them steaks.

For what was left of the night, I mostly tried to stay out of the way while I kept my ear to the ground about the status of the fires and any potential for gettin' out of town. As long as it was dark, I figured I could lie low enough in a busy, sleepless town such as Avery was into the wee hours of the morning. But when it got light, I knew, somethin' would have to be done, if the fires didn't force my hand sooner. For now, the Avery station was a crowded enough place, and it wasn't much effort to disappear into the woodwork, if no one in particular was lookin' for you. I sat down with my back to the station wall, on the track-side boardwalk. I was rubbin' shoulders with plenty of folk there, and no one paid me much mind. That situation changed soon enough, and before I'd had more than just a few minutes of wary sleep.

Before dawn this mornin', Sunday, August 21, the Palouser kicked up again. Word from down the line was that spot fires in the area of St. Marie's had by now joined, and spread to a breadth of nearly twenty miles! And it was all headed right in our direction. The speculators at the Restaurant were in for a sorry surprise. No rain would fall on these fires today, and this news would not depress the insurance rates.

I was still at the station when Debbitt and Deputy Sheriff MacMullen boarded a special engine West-bound. They were headed down to the area around Big Creek, to get a first-hand look at the fire front. Lieutenant Lewis of the 25th was left in charge of the situation in Avery, with the superintendent of the Milwaukee Road's Missoula division hoverin' close by, understandably nervous.

Before long, Avery was good and stirred up. Debbitt and MacMullen telephoned back from Big Creek that no time was to be lost in evacuatin' Avery. Winds in the St. Joe, they estimated, were hittin' seventy miles an hour, and the fires were bein' whipped into a holocaust capable of jumpin' the river and entire canyons. They told Lewis to get all the women and children out of town, and to let all others know to be ready to evacuate when notified. But to where, I wondered. I must say at this point that Lewis is a mighty fine man to have in charge under such pressure, and his troops prove most of what I've been told about Negroes to be lies.

The Milwaukee supervisor wasted no time in puttin' together two special trains, and sent the first up from the roundhouse. Within thirty minutes, Lewis had that train sent off loaded with just the women and children. Soldiers of the 25th were put at the doors of each car to keep things in control. Windows were fastened down and jammed with wet burlap, and every available bucket and barrel was filled with water and put on those cars. Lewis knew that the trestles up the valley had been burnin' since the day before, but the instructions for the engineers were to race for Missoula anyhow. They were only to stop if it became clear that the train would be trapped, wrecked and burned. In that event, the women and children were to be taken down into the river and kept from the embers as might best be done.

The engineer's strategy, as I understand it, was to wait for a flare-up to pass over the tracks, and then make a rush through after the peak of the flames. In this way, it might be possible to dash from one previously burned area to the next, while only gettin' heated up a bit and maybe scorched. The major risk in this gambit would be the burnin' trestles, and harm to the crews which had to clear debris from the tracks. Word got through this afternoon that these trains did make it out to Missoula. And we can thank God they did, especially after what I've seen today, and what I've lived through; and I fear the worst is still to come.

Men stood by (excepting fire-fighters, soldiers and Foresty-types) to board the second train out. And this is where things got chaotic.

I was sure enough glad to see the bulk of the 25th head out on the evacuation train, and happy that Debbitt and the Deputy Sheriff were out at Big Creek. But Lewis was organizin' crews to try to head off the fires West of Avery, and just as the second evacuation train rolls into the station, the Times reporter (Geiss) comes around with Lieutenant Lewis.

"Tad, here," says Geiss, tappin' me with his map case, "is an experienced man. He can lead your crew on Setzer Creek."

My God, I prayed. My heart was heavier than a lead ingot, and seemed to beat as slow as a death march. The Times man looked at me in a strange, hopeful way: like he wasn't sure about what he had told Lewis about me, but sure wished it to be true. It was as if he were testin' me.

"Is what this man tells me true?" asked Lewis. He was lookin' at me close in the murky dawn and oil-lamp light. There were sure-enough signs on me that I had already had some heavy experience with fire, and I could tell that Lewis was tryin' to make some connections that weren't quite clickin' yet. "Well, my name is Tad, sure enough. And yes," I said dryly. "I know what to do with a fire, and what to do with a crew." The truth was still of some use, even this morning, but what it was gettin' me into I had no idea. It was gettin' me out of town, though, and I thought that was good enough.

As the second evacuation train was bein' loaded, Lewis took me to the Avery Ranger Station, where I was introduced to a man named Rock. Two crews were bein' organized to set up fire lines on Setzer Creek, two miles West of Avery. Rock was headin' up the first.

If the fire could be stopped there, on Setzer, Debbitt had told Lewis, at the last significant canyon West of Avery, the town might be saved. (It was the rail yard, I reckon, that really wanted savin'.) Even if successful, though, there was still the fire comin' up the opposite bank of the river to worry about. But first things first.

Rock's crew was the first to be organized, and they set out up the trail to Wallace, hopin' to put in a line at the head of Setzer at Storm Mountain. I forget how many men Rock took with him, thirty or forty I think.

Lewis gave me eighty-two. We were to head down the tracks to Setzer Creek, and work a line up the length of Setzer to Rock's crew. My own crew was big, and they were already tired. It was hard gettin' 'em together.

"Listen up! Listen here," Lewis bellowed, gettin' the men's attention. The fellas weren't terribly happy about the relief train headin' out without 'em, and it was pretty noisy below the porch at the District cabin. Lewis stood up on the steps.

"I know things look pretty bleak today. And I know you're not at all pleased to be watching that train heading up the tracks. But you're not being asked to do something that those who lead you wouldn't do themselves."

There was some grumblin' at this, but Lewis went on.

"Ranger Debbitt himself is down at Big Creek this very moment, helping the crews that went out earlier this morning with Rangers Hollingshead and Bell. Deputy Sheriff MacMullen is with him, and they're both good men. What's more, they're closest to the worst of the fires right now. So when all's said and done, we're in the same boat together."

"That's just fine," one man said. "But we're just gettin' paid to do this, you know. We're not honest-to-god fire-fighters. Some of us were pulled off the rods down at the roundhouse, and others come out of the saloons. Why should we go out and risk our necks just for a few bucks we weren't really lookin' for in the first place?"

A few of the men hooted at this, and Lewis held up his hands. "All right. All right." Things quieted down. "Ranger Debbitt has asked me to assure you men that you will get paid, and that he'll do what he can to get you extra pay on top. But there is more to this than money. I know most of you men have nothing to protect here in Avery, and you're probably wondering why it is that those who DO are already on a train out of here."

"I'm not wonderin'!" one man hollered. "They're cowards!"

"If you want to talk about cowardice, we can," said Lewis, quieter. "I guarantee you I've seen cowardice, and I've seen bravery." And here he punched it out. "What I want to know is, what will I see here today!"

He stopped and looked sharply at the men, startin' to his left and movin' around the crowd, man by man, ending with me at his right. Things got mighty quiet. In his look there was fire, and there was challenge. Many men looked away.

"You don't know what the men on that train have to protect, nor do you know what's in their hearts. Their women-folk and children are on the train ahead of them. And yes, some of your own are on that train, too. Look at the men next to you." He paused. "Look at them!"

The men did as they were told.

"Today you'll be working alongside men you know nothing about. But by the end of this day, you'll know one thing: how you stack up in the eyes of the men beside you. Because you'll have done your duty, and you'll have done it well! That's why we do what we do: because we respect ourselves."

Lewis looked at me, and motioned for me to step up. I did.

"Tad here is an experienced man, and he's seen some intense action already this week. He can tell you what needs to be done. Tad?"

This caught me a bit off guard. I was not accustomed to public speakin'. I cleared my throat.

"Well, this is the story." I paused and looked over at Lewis, to my left. He nodded, and I spoke up a bit. "This is the story. Our crew and Rock's crew are headin' down to Setzer Creek. It's the last stand there for Avery, fellas. In all, they're askin' Rock and me to have you men cut over four miles of fire line, from river bottom to mountain top. We've got the entire ridgeline, boys, and I'll be there cuttin' with you."

I paused and looked back at Lewis, and Geiss was up on the porch with Sullivan, MacMullen's assistant Deputy. They were all lookin' at the men.

I continued. "You've all got some experience. I can see that. So time's a-wastin'. Let's get on down the tracks and lick this fire. I'll get you pointed in the right direction.

And I'll do what I can to lead you back."

There were a few natural leaders among that bunch, thank God, self-starters, and they started movin' out down toward the tracks. The men strung out a bit, and a few straggled; but they all went.

Lewis held out his hand. I don't know why, put I paused a bit before takin' it. I guess I had just never thought about takin' a soldier's hand before.

He held my hand firm. It was a good grip. "I don't know you from Adam, Tad. But I want to thank you."

"Sure," I managed, releasin' his hand.

"Do you believe in God?" he asked.

"I suppose I do," I says.

"On San Juan Hill," recalled Lewis, "Roosevelt said battle makes believers out of all men." He paused. "I think life's enough of a battle. Don't you?"

"I reckon," I agreed.

Geiss came down the steps to shake my hand as well, and Sullivan came with him.

"Can I get your full name for the paper, Tad?" Geiss asked as he took my hand.

"I don't reckon they need that information, Hod."

Sullivan put his hand on my shoulder. "People need a hero, Tad. Give 'em a hero with a name, why don't you."

I looked up at Sullivan. He seemed awfully serious. His eyes were clear and looked out of clean-shaven face, a rare sight in Avery that day. He was young, but had the feel of a much older man.

"My name's Roe. Thaddeus Roe," I says.

"Thanks, Tad," says Geiss, releasin' my hand.

Sullivan had not released my gaze. "Roe, huh?"

"That's right." I did not release his. "Roe. It's a name I'm proud to wear." And you know I am. I come by it honestly.

Sullivan stepped down and took Lewis by the arm. "I'm going with Tad, Lieutenant," he says. "I'll see what the lay of things are down on the Setzer and report back when they get under way."

Lewis nodded and looked back at me. I looked over at Geiss. He cocked his head a little, turned up one corner of his mouth and scratched the two-days growth of his chin with the butt of his pencil.

"I think we'll be all right here," Lewis says. "There's only a few men left now to keep track of."

"What about you, Hod?" I says to the reporter. "You want to join us?"

"Naw," he says. "I just cover the stories. I don't participate. Ruins objectivity." He laughed. "Bring me back a tall tale, why don't you?"

"Don't worry," says I. "I'll get legendary. Have no fear."

At that, Hod muttered some unintelligible noise, and I went off with Sullivan down to the tracks. We walked briskly and silently as far down as the roundhouse, trailin' the crew. We caught up to the rearguard about there.

Sullivan was at my side, and stopped me by puttin' an arm out in front of me. He was half a head taller than me, and well built (muscular, you know, and lean) so the gesture brought me up short. I looked him in the eye. It'd be a close thing figurin' who'd come out on top in a tussle between the two of us.

He took off his Stetson and wiped his brow with his sleeve. It was already gettin' mighty hot, early though it was still early. He held my eye.

"There's a yard full of cars and engines there," he says, and gestured over his shoulder. "You interested in takin' one, Monte?"

I'm pretty sure I blinked.

"If I tried, would I end up goin' out standin' up, or in a box?"

"Standin' up, I imagine," says Sullivan. "But I reckon I'd do my damnedest to put you in a box."

"And will you do your damnedest even if I don't?"

"I reckon that depends on you," he says.

My curiosity was piqued about as much as my ire was gettin' to be. I don't like fellas who beat around the bush.

"Well, this is how I see things, Deputy." I paused and licked my lips. "Do you mind if I wax eloquent for a minute?"

He tipped his Stetson back, and dipped some snuff. "Not at all," says he.

"Well, you obviously know who I am."

"That's right," says he. "Seen you once, down in Santa. And I've heard Pulaski talk about you."

"Then you know the stories, too."

"Yep," he nodded. "And I believe 'em about as much as I believe in Santa Claus. Stories start from some grain of truth, but along the way they get twisted a bit."

"That's true enough," I says. "Well, we ain't got all day to set the truth of all things straight, do we? And I can see you believe that, too. But one thing you do believe is that I'm better with a pistol than you are: and I probably am. You also believe that I don't carry my Colt strictly for my health, and I won't try to persuade you otherwise."

Sullivan spit to punctuate the point.

I continued. "What you're not sure of is this: that I'm a cold-blooded killer. And you're willin' to give me just enough rope to hang myself, in the interests of seein' what I'm made of. And if I turn out to be tin instead of iron," I says, lookin' down the tracks after the men, "if it's tin, you figger to be man enough to at least bring me up short, if not bring me down. Is that about the size of it?"

"Just about." Sullivan spit again.

"So how much rope are you givin' me?"

"There's a job to do," says Sullivan, "and it needs to be done. We don't have a lot of choices. Just do the job, and do it well."

"What's that mean," I asked, "in your opinion?"

"Put those men where they need to be, and do it responsibly." He paused, realizin', I think, that what he said didn't clarify things much. "I have no doubt," he continued, "that there's a good chance some of these men could die to today."

"I could, too."

"Yes, you could," says he. "Just make sure that if some of these men die, it's an act of God that does it, not an act of foolishness, carelessness or bad judgment. Or cowardice, or self-preservation. You're in charge. Prove to me that what most men say about you isn't true."

"And if I do?"

"No promises," he says. "I don't pull much weight in Avery. But I may keep my mouth shut about what I know."

"Do Geiss and Lewis know who I am, too?"

Sullivan looked away, and started walkin' again. "Pulaski said he worked with you on a fire once, and that you didn't seem to him like no damn cold-blooded killer. Said he knew your pa in Wardner, too."

It struck me funny at the time, but I wanted to use Hod's funny soundin' "A-ay-yuh," when he said that. I don't know why I did, but I did, and it made me laugh.

"What's so funny?" Sullivan asked. "Gettin' caught in a lie?"

"What lie?" I bristled.

"That your name is Roe. It isn't. You're Tad Montgomery, Ash's boy."

That made me mad. "I sure enough am. I'm also Three Card Monte, if anyone is. But my name's Thaddeus Roe. I don't have to prove it to you. And I don't care if you believe me. I know the truth, and that's enough for me."

"And the truth shall set you free, huh?"

John 8:32. I knew it well, but that was my business.

We walked on. It didn't seem I had much choice.

It was goin' to be a tough firefight, sure enough, and

the crews were made up entirely of paid volunteers—almost conscripts of a sort, mostly men who'd be run out of town on a rail if they didn't agree to work. There were some good honest townsfolk amongst 'em, but I'm pretty sure that in the whole bunch I saw there in Avery, only Rock himself was a trained Foresty man.

I wasn't one myself, of course, but I had done enough firefightin' over the last few summers that I knew well enough what needed to be done. About half a mile down the tracks, we caught up with the rear guard once more. Sullivan, who I take it had never been on a fire before, asked what I intended to do.

"Well, until I see the lay of the land, I don't rightly know for sure," I says. "But in general we can work from the presumption that the creek itself will form the beginnings of a natural barrier to the fire."

Now, in general, this was true. If things got as bad as they had the previous day on the Little North headwaters, of course, nothin' we could do would help. As some of the men were startin' to gather around and listen as we walked, though, I didn't want to get into what I'd been through the day before. It wasn't typical.

So I just went on. "The general strategy with a fire is this. Fire moves uphill quicker and easier than it moves downhill. You probably know that, and have seen that principle at work even in a simple camp fire."

"Well," says Sullivan, "that does seem obvious enough. But I do recall that I had to be taught that principle. I've had my share of camp fires go out because I'd forgotten that."

Talk seemed to be good for the men, who'd been trudgin' on in a pretty morose state. So I talked.

"If a fire is going to burn out, there's four ways for it to happen. The first is any kind of a barrier, say ten to twenty feet across. A stream bed is typically a good natural barrier, with the exception of the brush and downed snags that might allow the fire to jump the gulch. A fire line is a man-made barrier of the same sort."

"What about the water?" Sullivan asked.

I saw what he was gettin' at. "It's not the water in a creek bed that stops a fire, it's the lack of fuel for the fire. Rock won't burn. The spring current in a stream will strip the rocks bare of the leaves and needles that form the burnable duff you'll find on the rest of the forest floor, and smaller debris like branches just get swept away, swept aside. A fire line does the same thing: strips the ground bare, leaves no fuel. Dirt generally don't burn any better than rocks."

This was already far more speakin' at a stretch than I am normally wont to do. I stopped to breathe a spell, and took a drink of water from the canteen I'd picked up at the District cabin.

Sullivan filled the silence, which was good. "So I'm guessin' that the second way a fire will burn out is if it just loses momentum. Say, if the wind changes direction, or such like."

"That's right," I says. "Besides wind, another natural place for a fire to lose momentum is at the crest of a hill, or a ridgeline. Since we have no control over the wind, the two best ways to take advantage of that momentum-breaker are to either keep the fire from headin' uphill in the first place, or make it as difficult for the fire to advance downhill from a crest or ridgeline as you can. With the winds being what they are today, there's goin' to be no way of keepin' a fire from movin' uphill. Once a fire gets into the bottom of a canyon in these conditions, it will tear up the opposite side no matter what we do.

"So what we do is put a man-made barrier there at the crest: put a twenty-foot fire line in, four miles long, like I told the men back at Avery. And take the trees down there, too."

"Is that possible?" Sullivan was skeptical. "I mean,

can you do that in a day?"

"Well, again, that all depends on the lay of the land there. But yes, it's possible. I've seen a crew of fifty trained men put in a ten-mile fire line in a day."

One of the men nearby (Grogan was his name, an older fella, a good old gray-hair) chimed in. "But you said there was four ways to kill a fire. What's the other two?"

I imagine he was lookin' for an easier way than the one I'd sketched out for us. I didn't want to get his hopes up, so I told the truth.

"The easiest way (that is, the one that's the least work for us) is for Mother Nature to help with some rain. And it looks like that ain't goin' to happen today, I don't care how optimistic or hopeful any of you boys is. The fourth way, now, is dangerous, especially with winds like we've got today."

"Backfire," whispers another man.

"Yes, backfire," I says.

"I've heard of that," says Sullivan. "Burn the fuel that the fire wants before the fire gets there. Then there's no fuel left."

"That's right." I looked up the clouds of smoke unfurling up the valley from the leading edge of the fires now down at Big Creek. "It's the same principle, really, as a fire line: only you use fire itself to make it rather than the sweat of your brow and the ache of your back. It's a fire line, the quick, hot, deadly way."

I stopped, and now at the head of the group, I brought the men to a halt with me. We were at the mouth of the canyon. It was not yet quite mid-morning. The wind had picked up, so I spoke up as I concluded.

"And that's why a backfire is tempting: it's a lot less work, and takes less time. But it's also a last resort, especially in conditions like this, because it's hard to control. We won't backfire here unless we think we're going to be trapped. In that case, we'll fire the area between the creek and the fire line, and move into our backfired area once the flames clear it out. The main force of the fire may then either jump us, go around or burn out. But it's a desperate, desperate plan."

So I laid out the strategy for the men we would be using here: to try to keep the fire from headin' down slope to the creek, and using the creek itself as the final barrier. The going was going to be slow, as we had to cut our own trail up Setzer canyon. So the first thing to do was organize the trail detail. I put together three crews of axe men and two crews with saws. The timber was heavy around Setzer, but the gulch itself was relatively clear, with only scattered snags on the ground. The saw and axe crews would leap-frog each other, the axe men limbin' where necessary and workin' the smaller logs, and the saw crews cuttin' gaps in the bigger trees that couldn't be moved. I went at the front to blaze the path, and left twenty men at the rear to haul the remainder of the gear and our supplies for base camp as the trail was cleared. The balance of the men, about thirty, took spade and pick to actually clear the path.

This may seem like a lot of wasted work, but it's death to a fire crew not to have access to the area they're workin' in. Lack of communication and failure to get necessary supplies can be deadly. Of course, that's one of the problems with sendin' in firefighters to the St. Joe, Clearwater and Selway. The trails in these areas just don't exist. Sure, there's game trails: but they only take you where the deer want to go.

It took us near to two hours to clear the trail to a good base camp, about two miles up Setzer. The ground was steep, but not the worst I've seen for a fire line. I put half of the men who'd hauled the gear in charge of the camp, managin' supplies and cookin'. They'd taken the brunt of the first phase of the work, and some of 'em needed a breather.

I then split the crew into two major bodies. The smaller group, a crew of twenty-eight, I sent a mile or so above the main body: to work below Rock's crew and move down toward us. I put Grogan and another man named Blodgett in charge of the twenty-eight. Outflankin' the fire at its upper end, breakin' through to Rock's crew, was our best hope.

Now, it was unfortunate but true: the odds were good that we were facin' a crown fire advancin' towards us, in which case we were lost. But if it were a ground fire, advancin' with the wind across the sidehill, we might be able to stop it at the crest of the western slope of the Setzer with our fire line.

I stayed with the main body of the crew, now down to fifty-four, and strung 'em out across half a mile or so of the slope. Half were to work up toward our other twenty-eight, while the other half would work downhill. That put three fairly balanced crews each responsible for roughly three-quarters of a mile of fire line. When a crew finished a section, it could be moved down to the area below the lowest crew, allowin' us to leap-frog ourselves out of the canyon. This was a good, safe strategy.

I had the base camp crew get up some grub so it could be packed to the various crews as it was needed. By now it was gettin' on toward noon, and we were strung out over nearly two miles of canyon. Sullivan could see that things were organized and movin' well, so he took his leave. He didn't look back but once as he headed down the trail, and he didn't stop to do that.

I went up to join the center crew on the fire line to the West of Setzer. Each of the three crews had an axe team and two saw teams. At the crest of the ridge, everything burnable was stripped and flung back down into the gulch. The first task was to cut a swath twenty feet wide. The saw teams did this, and the axe team would follow to limb and clear up the smaller debris. Three or four men with peaveys would then get to ballin' the logs down into the gulch where possible, or harness up and haul 'em where it wasn't. Another five men worked the creek bed, gettin' it clear for the second fire break. The debris was hauled to the West bank.

Then the dirty work came: the fifteen or so remainin' men raked and spaded the debris and duff clean from the bare earth. Ordinarily, you'd get below the duff to some damp soil, which would be encouragin'. I hadn't seen that happen this summer, for some weeks now. So instead, you'd just peel the dry fuel back to leave bare, dry dusty earth in a twenty-foot band, snakin' through what must have looked like the path that Paul Bunyan's razor took across his huge hairy cheek.

We could have used old Paul today, and his Blue Ox too.

Saws were whippin', wood chips were flyin' and sweat was drippin'. The two lower crews were movin' at the rate of about a quarter of a mile an hour, good time; and yet it wasn't fast enough. The upper crew was havin' a tougher time, and hadn't met up with Rock's men yet, so they had begun to work uphill toward where Rock should have been. I was still with the middle crew. The sound of the fire advancin' on us was gettin' louder all the time, and it was gettin' darker. The ash was beginnin' to fall, just as it had done on the Little North the day before.

Sullivan soon arrived. It was about three in the afternoon. The roar of the oncomin' fire was now audible, like a towerin' wave of freight trains. He said something I couldn't hear, and yelled to repeat himself.

"It's a crown fire, and it's coming fast!"

I used some uncivilized language.

"Debbitt's afraid they've lost Hollingshead and Bell down on Big Creek."

That would be bad: thirty-five, maybe fifty men.

Sullivan yelled again. "Debbitt's sent word for you to

pull out as soon you're convinced the battle's lost here. He doesn't want another Big Creek. Get your crew back safe."

"I'll do what I can," I yelled back. "We'll come out as soon as it's clear the gulch has been jumped."

Sullivan took my arm. "The news is bad, Tad. The telegraph lines were up for while this afternoon. Word came in from Elk River that the men Lewis sent out after you yesterday have been lost. Four men, Tad."

My heart sank. "They were alive when I left 'em!"

"I believe you, Tad, I believe you. Just get this crew back safely to Avery."

Sullivan made his way through the debris piles and headed back across the Setzer. He hightailed it down to the trail. I had the axe and saw crews drop their gear, and detailed 'em off to fight the spot fires on the East bank of the Setzer that would soon be springin' up. We'd need the East bank for safe retreat down to the trail. There's no way we'd be able to fight our way down through the debris on the West slope.

Ralph, a lad with the crew who'd been fetchin' the men water, volunteered to head up the canyon to recall the crew of twenty-eight. He told me that the bulldog pup, which I'd left with my gear near the creek bed, had wandered off. I swore again.

The fire break we'd constructed at the ridgeline wasn't near wide enough, and it was incomplete. But it didn't matter. The fire had already flanked us by jumpin' the upper Setzer canyon, where it was narrower. The job was a loss. Not only that, it was going to turn fatal mighty quick.

As the river of flame from the racin' crown fire flooded and boomed over the ridge top, it wavered like an enormous saggin' orange wall, the heat beatin' down on us like a hammer amid rainin' embers and ash. The fire defied all experience and began movin' down the East bank from above, combustin' everything in its path by sheer heat alone. It didn't need spark to advance. Wind didn't matter. Slope didn't matter.

As I covered my head with my upraised arms and yelled to the men on the middle crew to get the hell out, I raced up the fire line as best I could to see what had become of the twenty-eight.

But the fire, which had easily jumped our upper line, was already racin' down the West bank toward the canyon floor. No, it rolled down the bank. It coiled like a prone funnel as the crown fire above and the flankin' fire on the West bank rushed to meet the fire now advancin' steadily down the East bank. Within steps, it was impossible to distinguish any line of fire in the canyon above me.

There was no line. Only fire. The twenty-eight were on their own.

I can only guess if they ever connected with Rock's crew, or what happened to 'em.

I turned to follow my men down the canyon, and vaulted the debris from the fire line to get to the canyon floor. I could see where the men I'd sent to the East bank had tried to kill spot fires. But hundreds more were springin' up. The heat had sucked every bit of moisture from the air, and it was scorchin' my lungs. I poured water from my canteen over my head as I ran, and doused the inside of my coat and pulled it over my face with one hand. I was grateful for the heavy gloves I'd borrowed for the day.

I hadn't gone far, maybe three hundred yards, when it became obvious that the same thing was happenin' at the lower end of the canyon as had happened above. I passed through the empty base camp, lookin' for the pup as I went, and hit the trail we'd made that morning. Thank God for the trail!

Cyclones of superheated air and flame stabbed down around me. If my men didn't get out now, they never would. I shielded my eyes the best I could and scanned the West bank for stragglers as I went. The nearest man to me was a hundred yards ahead, and there were no stragglers. The men had needed no motivation to flee. I could see 'em hurdlin' the flamin' snags that now began to crash down the slopes around us. It was a miracle no one was hit by the fallin' trees.

The lower end of the canyon was perhaps a quarter-mile or more across. And yet, incredibly, I could see that there was a continuous sheet of flame from rim to rim, towerin' maybe half a mile in the air. Two hundred yards ahead, vast arms of flame were moving down both slopes, cuttin' off our retreat. A hundred yards to go, and the last of my men were through. The gap was down to twenty feet or less. Fifty yards to go.

I didn't stop to see the escape route shut behind me. I might have had minutes to spare. It might have been seconds.

Men stood in shock on the railbed and stared back at the hillside above 'em. The flame and smoke were so thick you couldn't even tell where Setzer Creek had been. We stood or lay there, in shock, just prayin' for the fire to pass us by. Some men began to straggle weakly down to the river's edge And just as suddenly as the fire had overtaken us, evening came on and the wind died. Darkness fell, and many of the men with it. But all of the men on the lower crews were accounted for, and alive.

I got the men pulled together as best we could, and we staggered back into Avery, helpin' those too weak to walk on their own. Some men blubbered like babies, and I don't blame 'em one bit.

While my crew had been on Setzer, Debbitt and the Deputy had returned from Big Creek, as Sullivan had mentioned. Geiss had put his head together with Debbitt and Lewis to figure out that I was, in fact, Three Card Monte. They had never expected to see me come back from Setzer Creek, nor my crew.

They didn't know me.

Most of what they knew came from Geiss. The pony I'd brought into Avery had been found outside the Avery Hotel, and Geiss said he'd seen me lead it by the Hotel Idaho on my way into town. He told 'em I said I'd been on Slate Creek, and it wasn't hard for Debbitt to put two and two together from there.

MacMullen was waitin' for us out at the roundhouse, which was now all but empty. He's a rotund fella, and was bare-headed. Looked kind of funny. His top-knot was mostly bald: but just the top, and a clump of misplaced dark hair dangled from the front of his forehead, a forelock, really. Must have lost his hat down at Big Creek. He stepped out from behind a box car as we passed, his Smith and Wesson already drawn, and arrested me. I don't think any of the men noticed.

And it was plain to me, at least, that he did so reluctantly. I can only imagine he took pity on my burned and torn body. The soles of my store-bought work boots were nearly gone. If I'm gonna die with my boots on, I'd dearly prefer they be my Justins, and not these sorry things.

MacMullen took me first to the Hotel Idaho, without sayin' so much as a word. He hadn't even cuffed me, just asked for my gun belt, and then took me by the arm.

The men who'd been meetin' at the Hotel to decide on a course of action for the safety of those who remained in town, well, they had moved to the Avery Station while MacMullen was out. Sullivan remained behind, and told MacMullen he'd bring me along after cuffin' me. MacMullen went along to the Station.

"I'm really sorry about this, Tad," says Sullivan.

"We didn't all make it back, Deputy." My throat ached.

"Yeah, I know." He took my arms behind me, and

cuffed 'em. I asked for some water. He already had it ready, and I drank long and slow, with Sullivan's help, and then wolfed down a chunk of salt pork he stuffed in my mouth.

"You did good up there, Tad. No one's going to say a word against you for that." He doffed his 1100 Stetson and ran his hands through his hair. He was about as opposite a man from MacMullen as you could get.

"I lost twenty-eight men," I says.

"You don't know that, Tad, not yet."

I wondered what Debbitt would look like: dark and sallow, like MacMullen, or like some Celtic hero, like Sullivan? What kind of man would be responsible for sendin' me off to the Big Pasture?

"Look, Deputy. Just take care of my Colt for me, will ya?" I actually almost had tears come to my eyes. "It was my Daddy's, and it's been awfully useful to me over the years."

"I will, Tad, I will," said Sullivan. "But I don't think you'll be having much use for it from here."

That'd be true for a lot of things from this moment forward, I figured. And with that, Sullivan led me from the Hotel down toward the tracks and the Station. Debbitt took me aside and questioned me about what had happened on Slate Creek, and with Lewis's men on the Little North Fork. I didn't get real elaborate, but I told the truth, and the Times man was there takin' notes. Debbitt did not believe me. I think Geiss did; but it doesn't matter.

Debbitt then took me aside, and sent Geiss back to the conference. The Ranger wanted to talk to me alone.

Debbitt was an old-fashioned man, and old-guard to be sure. But not like Pulaski, Ed Thenon, and others of the old-guard type. He wasn't a local. He wasn't known in these parts. But he wasn't one of them Yale boys, either, or at least didn't seem to be. No, he'd seen some livin' somewhere, sure. You could just tell it about him. It was in the way he carried himself: not loose and confident, like most of these young Foresty boys, but tense and confident. Like he'd been through scrapes, knew he could get through more, and expected another one at any time. And he was weathered a bit, kind of like the bole of a young Ponderosa that's seen its own share of brush fires in its day. A survivor. The color is what mostly comes through, but if you look close you can see it's rough and blackened, a little hard.

So no, I don't reckon that Debbitt was much like Sullivan. No Celtic hero, no knight in shinin' armor here. No snatchin' victory from the jaws of death.

But no snatchin' death from the jaws of victory, either. Debbitt was a survivor. While MacMullen was desperate, and unsure of comin' out of this alive, and while Lewis was just confident in his duty (and his faith, I guess, bein' pretty much convinced they were one and the same) Debbitt was just constantly playin' the angles.

"You know," he says, "you just being here makes things mighty uncomfortable for me."

I knew how he felt, but wisely held my tongue, I think.

"And just so you know, boy, I don't give a rip about what happens to you."

Again, I could have assured him that the feelin' was somewhat mutual, given his attitude.

He went on. "I've been given a lot of men to manage here, and a lot of them are dying. In this district alone, we've got crews numbering upwards of eight hundred men. We're losing this battle, and now I've got Avery to contend with, too."

I pointed out that Lewis was doin' a right good job with the situation in Avery. This didn't seem to make Debbitt too pleased.

"Sure," he says, "sure, he's doing a FINE job. Like sending a wanted man off in charge of a crew of eighty-two, one of the largest in the district. Sure, a FINE job."

I think the pressure of the situation was gettin' to be a little much for Mister Debbitt. At this he grabs me by the collar and gets right in my face. His was not a face I wanted to be gettin' quite that close to. It was not particularly friendly.

"Look, now, kid," he snarls through his teeth. "You're a pariah. You're a Jonah. You're nothing but trouble, and misery follows in your wake. I've already got three warrants on you for murder, and now you've added four of my own men to the list."

I wanted really badly to point out that they were Lewis's men, and neither his nor his responsibility. But I bit my tongue. He was close enough I could have bit his, too. The urge did strike me, I must admit.

"If the twenty-eight men on Setzer are lost, like we think they are, they'll be on your head, too." And he relaxed here somewhat. "But you'll never know about that. You'll never know."

He pulled me over to a window and told me to look outside, across the street and tracks, down to the river.

"There's a town out there, son," Debbitt says. "It's got real things in it to worry about. Real things, and real people. It's martial law we've got on our hands here. Martial law. And when you run afoul of that, you go down.

"But just so you know" (and he turns back to face me here) "just so you know, your hours are numbered. I don't have the time to deal with you right now. You're a stone in my boot, and I'll tread on you. I will tread on you a bit more, before I pull you out and throw you away. But throw you away I will."

He paused here, but it didn't seem to me that he was askin' for input on this point, so I just nodded, sort of, and let things be. I knew well enough what he was sayin'.

But I guess he wanted to clarify things for me, just in

case the smoke had clouded my mind.

"I've got lives to save here, boy, and, well, yours just isn't one of them. I'm going to find some real secure place for you, you can bet. And if you're still around when this is all over, you can guarantee yourself that martial law will fall, and it will fall hard."

I did speak up here. "I don't suppose there's anything I could do or say that would change your mind about that?"

He just looked at me with that, and started to walk away. Now, he hadn't at all spelled out what he had in mind for me. But he made it clear, then, when he turned around and looked at me with derision. "Horse thief," he says.

Now, I don't suppose that really meant all that much to him, really. But then again, maybe it did. He'd been around, and seen some, so maybe his people had been horse or cattle people, too. But the point was, he knew what that meant to me. So he knew he could tell me what he had in mind, without just comin' out and sayin' it. He could threaten me, without anyone bein' able to say that he'd threatened me, exactly.

Debbitt was sayin' that if I survived the fire, they were almost sure to hang me.

I think the irony of the situation was lost on Debbitt: that as he left me with that news, he was returnin' to the meetin' they were havin', a meetin' to figure out how best to save the lives that remained in Avery.

At Debbitt's and MacMullen's suggestion, it was decided that it would be best to try marchin' up the St. Joe valley to reach areas which had already been burned out. What wind there still was had now shifted and was blowin' the fires up and over the hills toward Wallace. But that was blowin' the fires which were to the South of the St. Joe right toward the river and Avery. The remains of the Setzer Creek blaze were advancin' slowly but steadily as well. It was generally agreed that Avery would be a total loss.

But MacMullen knew that he really had no authority in Avery. It was a company town, and there was really no law but temporary martial law, and unofficial at that: not even a jail. So Debbitt prepared to lead those who would follow him, and the rest were given permission to attempt whatever escape they wished. Geiss said he would remain in Avery to document its demise, and regretted havin' no photographic equipment with him.

They even asked me what I preferred to do, seein' what I'd been through, and that I was not in much shape to travel. Now, this was not Debbitt's idea, but Lewis's. I told 'em that if it was all the same to them, I'd as soon try my luck in Avery. If I survived, they could hang me, or do what they would. I was done runnin', especially from fires.

They took me back to the Hotel Idaho, lockin' me inside the vault's cage. The Times man (that is, Geiss), he took the keys, and agreed to vouch for me. Debbitt seemed happy enough with this arrangement. MacMullen didn't seem to care.

The infirm and the old men were then taken to an old mine shaft somewhere on the edge of town, I'm not sure where. It might have been the adit with the piano. But Geiss says, wherever it was, it was stocked with provisions and covered with wet blankets. It seemed safe enough for those who couldn't travel, I guess, but Debbitt, Lewis, MacMullen and Sullivan led the bulk of the men up the St. Joe on foot. To me, this seemed kind of irresponsible.

It also proved ill-advised. They had gone maybe half a mile when it became clear that escape would not be possible in that direction, at least not on foot. At that point, one group of men came back and took a train East, although it had become well known during the day that all the bridges in that direction, and many of the tunnels, were impassable. Nonetheless, they thought they might have a chance of breakin' through to the old burn from the 17th, and ridin' out the fires there.

Debbitt, in the meantime, was preparin' to take a small group of men into the river with blankets for protection. Lewis disagreed with this strategy strenuously. While the St. Joe is mostly shallow in other places, the eddies and pools alongside Avery were too deep, he thought, and more might drown than die of fire elsewhere. With MacMullen and Sullivan, Lewis led the bulk of the men West on the last engine remainin', equipped only with one flat-car and a box. During the day, the roundhouse had been emptied of all other cars, which had been sent to the burn-out East of Avery to save 'em from the fire they knew would take Avery.

So for the last several hours, no more than six or seven men have remained here in Avery. Hod Geiss, from the Times, has been with me here in the Hotel vault, readin' these pages as I complete 'em. He's been takin' down a good deal of it, too, shorthand. Debbitt has sat by some, but mostly goin' in and out, and I do not think he has been much impressed. But he's pretty chafed, what with the bulk of folks followin' Lewis and not him.

But here's the thing: I have told the truth, and I am innocent. But I remain in chains.

Debbitt has said he plans to backfire the town sometime early this morning, and has just left to round up whatever men he can find for the job. In theory, if the out-buildings on the West end of town can be burnt safely, the advancin' fires will find no purchase, and may spare the remainder of the town.

It is likely a vain hope. Geiss can see embers already fallin' on articles of furniture in the street, left there by residents thinkin' their belongings might survive the burnin' of their homes. The stuff may end up burnin' faster out there on the street.

Geiss promises to do what he can to transcribe his notes, and maybe even manage to get this letter to you. It's a stack of paper, sure.

If I survive the night, consider this document my testament, and do not believe the stories they tell. If I do not survive? Well, consider me no more. I beg you.

In any event, I pray you will not believe the legend of Three Card Monte. I would always have you remember me as

A son of my Father,
Thaddeus Roe.

Avery, Idaho
Tuesday, August 22, 1910

PEACEMAKER

(From the Seattle Sunday Times, *August 28, 1910)*

AVERY MAN TELLS HIS EXPERIENCES IN HELL OF FIRE
Was Leader of Band of Eighty-two Fire Fighters,
of Whom Twenty-four Perish, Hemmed in by Flames
WARM WORDS OF PRAISE FOR COLORED SOLDIERS
Black of Skin, but White of Heart, and Gallant,
Loyal Workers—Pathetic Incident of Death of Terrier

The first man to reach the outside world from Avery, Idaho, since the fire that cost the lives of twenty-four men, Thaddeus A. Roe, forest ranger, is in Seattle with the details of the battle for life, fought by eighty-two men against the ring of flamc that surrounded them August 22. With no outside point was communication possible until the first train reached Avery August 23 and the published stories of the fate of the men at Avery have been incomplete.

With eighty-two men under him Roe advanced up Setser Creek on the morning of August 22 to face the almost hopeless task of controlling the flames that the big wind of the night before had fanned from smoldering ashes into a hell of fire. A line of flames six miles long was burning to the north of the band of men who advanced up the canyon making their own trail as they moved. The ends of the fire line were slowly closing in behind them and the forlorn hope was to break through the column of flame in front. Twenty-four of the men were detailed to this work while fifty-eight remained in the rear to keep open the only remaining avenue of escape.

Sent Boy with Warning.

At 4:00 o'clock in the afternoon Roe saw that the work was futile and sent Ralph Waters, employed as a water boy, up the creek to inform the vanguard of the fire fighters that they must turn back at once in order to save their lives. Waters never came back. Next morning Roe and the searching party found his body in the little stream where he had sought refuge. Farther up the canyon, within a radius of thirty feet the bodies of the twenty-four men were found.

After dispatching Waters up the valley Roe realized it was useless for his party to remain longer in the fire zone, and then began a race with the flames. The fire was sweeping down the sides of the canyon and the opening between the two fires was narrowing each minute. The men had two miles to go before they reached the spot where the two fires would meet eventually. It was a question whether or not they would pass through this rapidly narrowing gap before it closed and shut off the only road of retreat. Forcing their way along the trail they had hurriedly created the previous night, the exhausted force ran stumbling towards the opening in the distance. When a man fell his companions dragged him along nearer the goal.

SORROW OVER COMRADES' FATE.

When the red-eyed, gasping fire fighters at last crawled through the opening into the zone of safety beyond, the aisle untouched by the fire was less than a quarter of a mile wide.

It was impossible to turn back, for in an instant the two fires had met and the twenty-four men far up the canyon were completely surrounded. Joy at being safe was completely drowned by the thought of the fate of their comrades, and the men stumbled slowly back into camp with bowed heads.

Roe, alarmed at the unhalting progress of the fires, made his way into Avery, and that night, together with eight of the businessmen of the town, back-fired, saving almost single-handed the portion of the town which is standing today. William Lynch, Edward Bussett, James Sheehy, Lee Setser, Archie Lane, Frank Delamater and James Roberts, of all the inhabitants of Avery, remained behind to protect the town with Roe.

Avery is situated in the heart of a little circular canyon, and when the little force began to back-fire at 11 o'clock that night the fire they were trying to stand off had already crossed the crest of the hill a half mile away.

The story is best told in Roe's own words:

"In order to save anything at all we had to begin firing the buildings on the outskirts of the town, and then the terrible work of forcing the back-fire towards the big blaze began. I will never forget the sight. An impassable wall of fire was eating its way down the hillside. Our back fire, which had assumed huge proportions, was creeping up towards it. In exactly four and one-half minutes after we had started our fire the two met. Never have I seen anything like it. Plunging at each other like two living animals, the two met with a roar that must have been heard miles away. The tongues of fire seemed to leap up to heaven itself, and after an instant's seething sank to nothingness.

"We had won, but the strain of those four and one-half minutes had exhausted us and we sank to our feet and lay there in the ashes babbling incoherent thanks to God.

"The rest of the world didn't know what we were going through. It couldn't, and that was the terrible part of it. We might have been the only men in the world for all it mattered. Alone we were left with nothing but our bare hands and the help of our Creator to bring us through alive."

SEARCH FOR DEAD COMRADES.

The morning following thirty-four of the fifty-eight men who had miraculously escaped the day before, together with Roe and twelve members of Company G, Twenty-fifth (colored) Infantry, began the tedious and heart-breaking effort to cut their way through the charred mass of fallen logs that rose between them and their dead companions. Foot by foot they wormed their way through the still smoking territory.

Though they were prepared for it they suffered a terrible shock when they came upon the first body. It was that of Patrick Grogan, a light-hearted Irishman who had been the life of the camp the day before. This was one of the only two bodies identified. The other body, that of James Blodgett, was the last to be discovered.

The negro troopers dug a sixty-foot trench in the warm ground and the bodies, stitched in canvas and bearing tags with numbers showing the order in which they were found, were laid to rest. The twelve soldiers fired a volley over the open graves and when the dirt had been thrown in the brawny bugler played "Taps," the "lights out" of the army camp.

"I want to tell you something that happened," said Roe in his narrative last night. "I had taken a little bulldog, a bright little one I called Rox with me when I went to Avery to take up the work of controlling the fires.

Just Plain Dog, But—

"Rox took a big interest in everything that went on about the camp, but was a little too enthusiastic and to keep him from crawling into my makeshift bunk at night I built a little corral and penned him up in it.

"Just after we had buried the boys, the negro bugler found what was left of poor Rox.

"'Boss,' he said to me, 'my conscience wouldn't be clear if I left without doing things up right for the little fellow.'"

Digging a little hole in the ground, they

tenderly laid Rox into it, and when it had been filled the bugler stood up and slowly played "Taps."

As the notes of the bugle swelled and reverberated through the denuded hills about them these two strong men stood with the tears rolling down their cheeks as they gazed out over the grave of Rox—plain dog, who simply died.

"I will never forget the little scene," said Roe. "If I had laid my own child away that day I would not have felt more grief."

Negroes With Hearts of Gold.

"I want to say something about those negroes now. They were black, but I never knew a whiter set of men to breathe. Not a man in that lot even knew what a yellow streak was. Brave? We Anglo-Saxons don't even know what it means. If being flayed alive would make them white skinned there isn't a man of them that wouldn't stand it with closed lips.

"In the heat of the day, in the middle of the night, they worked under my direction. They never complained. They were never afraid. They worked, worked, worked like Trojans and they worked every minute. I can't say too much about them but I will say that my attitude towards their race has undergone a wonderful change since I knew those twelve black heroes."

Roe also explained the reason for the sudden progress made by the flames August 22nd.

"A big windstorm sprang up on the night

of August 21," he said, "and the fires, which had been smouldering in scattered fashion through the woods, were fanned into new life. We were fools to endeavor to cope with the ten-mile line of fire that encircled the curved valley of Setser Creek, but it was our duty and we couldn't turn back with consciences clear."

ROE'S BODY MASS OF BURNS.

"We had no adequate idea of the extent of the flames at first, for we could not realize what had transpired in the course of a single night. The scattered fire had united into one impregnable circle about us. It was a death trap, and I thank God alone that I am here to tell you the story."

When Roe reached Avery on the night of the day when twenty-four men met death his outer garments had been burned from his body. His heavy woodman's boots had been burned through, and only a remnant of a hat hung over his scorched head. His arms and legs were a mass of burns, the scars of which he will carry to his grave.

Roe was thirty-two years old when he went into Avery six weeks ago. Today he looks like a man of fifty, and gray has marked his hair. He will never be able to tell many of the things he saw in the last ten days near Avery, after the town had been deserted, for the story would not be an entertaining one to listen to. Locked up in his heart is a story of hardship and bravery which he would never care to share with another.

Monday Roe will return to Avery to take up his work where he dropped it several days ago.

In speaking of the way in which The Times handled the story of the disaster Roe said:

"I cannot understand how The Times managed to do what it did. It is simply marvelous. I was astounded to pick up Tuesday's copy of your paper and see the picture of myself and my men taken on the morning of the day we started up Setser Creek.

"The information you conveyed to the public is absolutely accurate as far as I can gather from a careful reading of all the copies of your paper which appeared since the day of the disaster."

The following deposition of
JOHN WILLIAM (JAYDUB) REDEYE, homesteader,
was taken before
Phyllis M. Bedynek, Certified Court Reporter and Notary Public in the State of Idaho.

APPEARANCE OF COUNSEL
On behalf of Darrow and Associates: MR. JAMES B. SLAUGHTER.
On behalf of The State of Idaho: MR. KENNETH MERCKX.

In the following transcript, a dash (—) at the end of a statement is used to indicate an unintentional or purposeful interruption in a sentence; a bracketed ellipsis ([...]) is used to indicate omitted words, such as profanity; and a simple ellipsis (...) indicates halting speech or an unfinished sentence in dialogue or an omission of word(s) when reading written material. Descriptions of actions are noted parenthetically.

DISCLOSURE

I, Phyllis M. Bedynek, am present for the taking of this deposition called upon today only; there is no discount arrangement existing between any party to the deposition and the reporter; there is no referral from someone with a contract for the reporter taking this deposition, or otherwise; I am not kin nor counsel to parties involved in this deposition; and I am not interested in the outcome of any possible case in which this deposition might be submitted as evidence. This thc 12th of December, 1910.

(Witness sworn.)

JOHN WILLIAM (JAYDUB) REDEYE having been first duly sworn, was examined and testified as follows.

EXAMINATION BY MR. SLAUGHTER:

Good morning, Mr. Redeye. My name is James Slaughter. I represent Darrow and Associates and will be conducting the deposition this morning. I appreciate you allowing us to come here at this early hour to get going.

I reckon you should.

Mr. Redeye, have you ever given a deposition before?

Not that I would know of. Should I have?

I'm sure I wouldn't know. I'm going to give you some instructions about how this deposition will proceed. You're under oath now and your testimony carries the same weight and importance as if you were a witness at trial. The testimony that you're giving in this deposition can be used at trial if any case related to the matters in question should ever proceed to trial. Your testimony in this deposition is part of a public record and the transcript of this deposition could be freely disseminated and discussed.

What the hell does that mean?

I'm sorry?

Disseminated. What the hell are you getting at?

That means distributed. The things you say are being written down, and might get around.

Oh. Well, I damn well hope they do.

Regarding the questions that we're going to ask you, you must answer each question fully and completely. If you don't understand a question, please ask me to clarify the question. If you go ahead and proceed to answer, we'll assume that you understand the question and are able to answer it fully and completely.

That's mighty big of you.

From time to time, Mr. Merckx, here, may feel a legal need to lodge an objection to the form of a question that I ask, or a statement that I make. That objection is solely to make a legal record for consideration later on if Mr. Merckx so chooses. You're to go ahead and answer a question, or respond to my statement, even if Mr. Merckx objects—that is, unless he gives you some type of specific instruction in that regard.

What about me?

What about you?

What if I object to the form of a question?

Well, just let me know and I'll apologize to you.

Yeah, well, you damn well better.

Mr. Redeye, we're going to start with some background information before we get into the merits of your opinion in this case. Have you brought any materials with you to the deposition today?

Huh? What's that? Brought anything? I'm in my own damn house.

Yes, sir, of course. I'm sorry. The question is a matter of formality, and I simply forgot where I was.

Well don't be so formal, son. You're confusing the hell out of me. And by the way, you're the ones who decided that my opinions, as you call them, pull some weight in this case. So don't be going and giving folks the impression that somehow I think my opinions are so all-fired important.

Yes, sir. I'm sorry.

That's all right. It's just that if you're going to go spreading this here talk around, I want that clear.

Certainly. Now, for the record, could you please tell me your name, and describe your place of residence.

You know my dad-gum name.

Yes sir. This is just for the record, so that folks who read the record know something about you.

My name's Jaydub Redeye and—

Excuse me, sir. Is Jaydub your given name?

Well, I reckon someone give it to me at some point. I weren't born with it.

Yes sir. What name were you born with?

I weren't born with no name. No one is, dad-gum it.

No sir, I suppose not. What was the name given to you by your parents?

My papa was an Indian by the name of Redeye. When I was born, my mama—she was a Catholic white woman, and she... uh... spent some time amongst the Indians—well, she had a priest christen me John. My papa said if he was going to call me by a white man's name, it would be William. So they split the difference and called me John William Redeye. As long as I can remember, though, folks have just called me Jaydub.

Thank you. And could you describe for me your place of residence?

Well, it's a pretty good piece of ground. I got me a quarter section of bottom land, and I've proved up on it sure enough. I don't cotton to timber cruisers and I can show you the land I've cleared if you want to see it. I've been breeding horses and truck farming for fifteen years now, and—

Thank you Mr. Redeye. But I was asking—

I know dang well what you were asking, son. And I bet I know something you don't.

What's that, Mr. Redeye?

That horse manure accumulates at the rate of five tons per animal per year.

Is that right?

Yes, sir, that's right. And I've got a lot of horses. So I know something about horse manure. Now, do you want me to answer your question fully and completely, or don't you?

Yes sir, of course.

All right then. I got horses, truck, and I got a few head of cattle. Mostly, though, I raise horses. The Bull River is good country. I've been on the Bull for nigh on to twenty-five years, one way or another. I come to the area first in 1888, prospecting. I didn't find no gold, but I sure found I liked the land.

And where is the Bull River, exactly?

Well, dang, boy. Ain't you got eyes?

Yes sir. Of course. I meant, could you describe for the record where your homestead on the Bull River is located, and what towns, valleys and such are nearby?

My spread is about ten miles up Lake Creek from Troy, which sits on the Kootenai River in Northwestern Montana. It's just below Bull Lake, which is what I mean by it being on the Bull River.

Could you clarify that for me, please?

Well, Bull Lake is at the top of the divide between the Kootenai and the Clark Fork. The Cabinet range divides the two. Now, Bull River runs out of Bull Lake, which sits in a low spot at the Cabinets, and the Bull runs down into the Clark Fork just below Heron, where the ferry is. My spread's just the north side of Bull Lake, and on that end the drainage is Lake Creek. And it runs down into the Kootenai at Troy. There's a ferry there, too. But folks around there refer to the whole valley up here as the Bull River.

What other towns are close by?

Not much, really. Besides Heron and Troy, there's just Libby, which is a few miles upriver from Troy.

Thank you. And where is the area in which you lived prior to homesteading on the Bull River?

Well, I was at what's now Wardner when the Bunker Hill ledge was found in '86, and then I spent some time near Lee's Cabin up Cherry Creek, above what's now called Libby. It was a mining supply camp in them days. From there I spent some time near what used to be Sylvanite, before it burned last August. That's on the Yaak.

Could you tell us how you are familiar with the man known as Three Card Monte?

Why, the same as most folks, I guess. Stories get around. Rumors and such.

But you knew him personally, didn't you?

Can't say as I did.

You didn't know Tad Montgomery?

Sure I did. That's not what you asked. You asked if I was familiar with the man called Three Card Monte.

To your knowledge, aren't Tad Montgomery and Three Card Monte the same man?

Well, now, I don't think I'd say that at all.

Why not, Mr. Redeye?

Three Card Monte's a lot like Buffalo Bill, if you know what I mean. He's a fella that people will tell stories about just to be telling stories. You know, if it hadn't been for the fires last August, I would have gone into Seattle to see Buffalo Bill. That I would.

Buffalo Bill was in Seattle? No kidding.

Yep. And that's the end of an era, sure enough. It was his farewell tour with Pawnee Bill and the whole bunch. I sure enough would have liked to have seen that.

I'm sure. So you wouldn't say that you ever met Three Card Monte?

Mr. Merckx: Objection. Mr. Redeye, don't answer that question.

What the hell's so objectionable about that question?

Mr. Merckx is just making a formal record of the fact that he doesn't care for the way in which I worded the last question.

Well, hell, you didn't curse or nothing.

No sir, I didn't. Let me ask the question in a different way. In your mind, is there such a man as Three Card Monte?

Well, in my mind there just might be, sure enough. But in my mind, I may be the Sultan of Egypt, too. So I'm not sure what significance there might be to what's in my mind. But if you're trying to suggest, as a lot of different folks have, that Three Card and Tad are one and the same fellow—well, I sure ain't having none of that.

Why not?

Well, listen up. This here is what I've heard about Three Card Monte. He's a hair-trigger gunman. He's a thief. He's a murderer. He's a card-sharp, a whoremonger, and a claim-jumper. He could shoot your eye out at fifty yards from his hip, and would just as soon spit in it afterward. He's an ornery cuss if there ever was one. Now, Wyatt Earp himself was Sheriff over in Kootenai County in Idaho in 1883— You know who he is?

Yes, Mr. Redeye, I'm familiar with Mr. Earp.

Not too familiar, I hope, for your sake. Well, now, Wyatt Earp himself was a County Sheriff in these parts, and I hear tell he even ran the White Elephant Saloon in Eagle City. Mr. Earp, now, he might have actually run up against a character like Three Card Monte in his day. Sure enough. And if he had, it might have been interesting to see who'd have gotten the best of who. But me— Now me, I've never seen the likes of such a legend. No sir.

Could you tell me what you know about Tad Montgomery?

Well, now there's not much to tell about that, but if you want to know something interesting, you might be interested to know that Mr. Earp undoubtedly knew Tad's pa, old Ash Montgomery, over in Eagle City. That's an interesting fact. And I could tell you some stories about old Ash.

Thank you, but no, that will not be necessary today. But why do you say there's not much to tell about Tad Montgomery?

Well, because Tad was just a boy before he went away. He was just ten, I think, or thereabouts, when the Fewkes boys shot up and burnt down his daddy's place on the Kootenai, and his momma died. When old Ash made that mess of Billy Blew's place in Libby, that left Tad an orphan. He lived for a few years with an old man there at Ash's place, and was sent away long about the time he was sixteen or so. I forget precisely. So all I knew of Tad was that he was one of the younguns hereabouts. I saw him from time to time at camp meetings and such, but didn't know much other than he was pretty handy with a pistol. Always was.

Are you familiar with the name Thaddeus Roe?

Well, yes, I suspect I should be. I see what you're doing, now. You're asking me stuff that you already know I know.

Yes sir, I suppose that's a good description of what we're doing. Are you familiar with newspaper reports about Thaddeus Roe?

Well, I haven't read them myself, but I am aware of them, yes.

Can you tell me what you know about the newspaper reports?

In general, I consider newspaper reports pretty unreliable. Entertaining, but pretty unreliable.

Well, I specifically wanted to know what you know of the newspaper accounts of Mr. Roe.

Oh. Well, the newspapers make him out to be a hero or somesuch—which is pretty interesting, considering that there's a lot of other folks who want to make Tad out to be the one and the same villain that Three Card Monte is supposed to be.

So you know that Three Card, Tad Montgomery and Thaddeus Roe are purported to be the same man?

Purported to be—what's that mean?

Ostensibly. Said to be, whether or not it's true.

Whether or not it's true? Well, sure. Everyone knows that Three Card Monte is supposed to be one and the same as old Ash's boy.

So, what can you tell me about what you know of Thaddeus Roe, the hero, from the newspaper reports?

Mr. Merckx: Objection.

He objected to that hero part, didn't he?

Please answer the question, Mr. Redeye.

Well, like I says, from what I gather, the papers make him out to be some kind of hero, like you says. Hero.

Do you read, Mr. Redeye?

Well, no, I don't reckon I do.

Then how do you know what the papers have to say about Thaddeus Roe?

From what other folks have read to me. I think upwards of fifteen people have read at least some part of that article to me. It says that Thaddeus led a crew of firefighters, somewheres down Avery way, and then almost single-handedly saved the entire town. And there's a bunch of hen squawking about colored folks. It's about as bad as the stories about Three Card Monte.

Could you explain why you say that?

Well, the Three Card stories which I have heard are just about the kind of outrageous tall tales that folks want to tack onto a man, in a bad way. You know, whether or not they belong there. And it's easy, like swimming downstream, or slapping your kids. You don't have to stretch much when the truth has already been stretched. But the newspaper stories about Thaddeus go almost the opposite direction, and it's a bit like swimming upstream, or not slapping your kids when you want to—pretty tough. It's like they're trying to carve a hero out of soggy sourdough.

How so?

Okay, well, here's a few things. First off, Thaddeus Roe was not in Seattle talking to a reporter on the 27th of August, or anywhere thereabouts.

How do you know this?

Because he was put in a box in Libby on the 25th.

Put in a box?

Dead. That's the only way you get into a box.

Did you see him dead?

No, but plenty of folks did.

Where were you on the 25th?

In a cabin down on the Kootenai, nursing these here bullet holes you see.

Do you have information which would support the claim that Thaddeus Roe died in Libby on the 25th of August, 1910?

You mean, as opposed to being in Seattle on the 27th?

Yes, that's right.

Yes. I saw him well nigh all day on the 24th. I drank with him, and I fought beside him. In my book, that would pretty much support a claim that he was in these parts, at least.

Thank you. Can we return to the newspaper reports, for a moment? You remarked that the stories in the paper seem manufactured to you. What else strikes you as false about those reports?

Well, some of the things that Thaddeus is reported to have said—the quotes, you know, that they use in the piece—some of the things they say he said do sound like Thaddeus, sure enough. But others just don't.

Could you elaborate?

Well, I suppose I could belabor it for you a bit, sure. The remarks about colored folks, for instance. That sounds like Thaddeus. Simple, straightforward, thoughtful. The other stuff don't—like the business about the dog. And that stuff at the end, singing the praises of the paper and the reporter. I don't think that's so. I think the reporter made that stuff up, and it was easy to because that fella Thaddeus that he was making up weren't there.

Can you speculate about why the reporter would want to make stuff up, as you say?

Mr. Merckx: Objection. Mr. Redeye, you may answer the question, but let the record show that Mr. Redeye's answer constitutes speculation.

So noted. Mr. Redeye?

Well, now. That's a pretty fine how-do-you-do, ain't it? It's pretty fun seeing you boys dance a little. You want some pistols?

The question, if you please, sir.

Well, I liked Mr. Merckx's word there—speculation. Because that's what papers do a lot of the time, don't they—speculate? So let me speculate as to why. First, it could be they don't have the facts, and that's a tough nut because folks expect them to. But they often enough don't seem to have the facts, do they? Second, it could be because they don't like the real facts, the facts the way they actually happened. Or third, it could be because they want to manufacture their own facts. In this case, I think it's probably some combination of the second and third cases, there.

Why?

Well, there's a lot of people who died down there around Avery, aren't there?

Yes, there are.

And someone's got to be responsible, don't they?

I suppose so, yes.

MR. MERCKX: Objection. Don't respond, Mr. Redeye.

What do you mean, Mr. Redeye?

Well, let's just say that a couple dozen men die in a fire—just to speculate like. I don't want to let on like I actually know nothing or anything. Now, a lot of folks want to know why those couple dozen men—or maybe it's twenty-eight—they want to know why those men died. And some of those folks who want to know why, well, they're folks who are taking some serious heat from some other folks who are already taking some serious heat. Well, [...] rolls down hill, don't it?

For the record, let it be stated that Mr. Redeye's colorful language will be stricken. Mr. Redeye, if you could please refrain from language which the lady might find objectionable.

Well, that tells you something about the lady, doesn't it? I'll just say it the way I already said it earlier, and you didn't catch it. The Bull runs down to the Clark Fork, don't it?

I'm sorry?

What I'm getting at is that it's pretty easy to pin those two dozen deaths on a man who's no longer alive, isn't it? But if someone else was really to blame, someone who's trying to avoid responsibility, it'd sure be nice to clear the name of an innocent man, wouldn't it—or at least, to shift blame elsewhere? If Thaddeus Roe is the hero of Avery, he can't very well be the villain of Setser Creek, can he?

You said, Mr. Redeye, that you believe the published reports about Mr. Roe were either false in some respect because the real facts aren't palatable, or because an invented story might be more useful. Wouldn't the presence of unfactual information in the account shed some doubt upon the heroism of the subject of the account?

If you mean—don't a few lies mixed in with some truth discredit the truth altogether? Then, no. I don't think so. You know, I don't disbelieve the part about raising from the dead, you know, simply because one scribe says the teacher cast demons out of two fellas and another scribe says it was just one. Other facts need to be considered.

You don't think the entire account is fabricated?

No, I don't.

Are you of the opinion that the reporter's account is based in fact?

Yes, I reckon that the reporter at least spoke to Thaddeus—that, is he sure enough spoke to Tad. Now, his article—it sure as hell ain't inspired, if that's what you mean. But I doubt that the reporter actually saw what he reported, or heard what he said he heard. Like I was sayin' about the dog. There was a dog, sure enough. But Thaddeus wouldn't have talked about it like the reporter has him doing. That's awfully [...] flowery. Taps, and the tears and all. The stirring words from the buffalo soldier.

It's too much—good for rousing up the ladies and such, I reckon, begging your pardon, ma'am, but not too good a portrait of Thaddeus.

You say there was a dog. How do you know?

Because Tad told me.

Thaddeus Roe told you.

Well, after a manner of speaking, yes, I guess that's a fact.

How did he tell you this?

Well, with words, you know. Face to face. We talked.

How many times did you talk with Thaddeus Roe last August?

Just the once. But it lasted a good long spell.

Earlier you said you saw Mr. Roe on the 24th of August, 1910. Is that when he spoke to you about the dog?

Yep. That would have been it. And it were.

And did he speak to you of other subjects than the dog?

Oh, yeah. Sure. Bundles of stuff.

Can you tell me where this conversation with Mr. Roe took place?

I was at the Bull River Ranger Station with Charlie Dennis. It's just a short piece from here. Charlie, he's the head of the Troy District of the Cabinets. We'd been over mopping up at Sylvanite the day before and had come back just that morning. Tad came up the Bull River wagon road long about ten that morning.

Do you recall if Mr. Roe mentioned the names Debitt, McMullan or Sullivan?

Not off hand, no.

Do you recall if Mr. Roe mentioned the Forest Ranger at Avery?

Yes, he did talk about a ranger. I didn't catch the name, though. I suppose it must have been—what did you say? Sullivan, or Debitt or McWhatsit.

McMullan.

Right.

Do you recall if Mr. Roe mentioned the presence of Deputy Sheriffs at Avery?

Oh, yeah. They were there.

Mr. Redeye, we're particularly interested in what transpired on the day that Mr. Roe left Avery. Can you tell us what day that was?

Well, I spoke with Tad on the 24th. The previous night he'd been into Heron. On the 23rd, then, he would have been through Evolution and Eagle City. Or thereabouts. He would have left Avery on the 22nd.

Not the 23rd?

Wouldn't have been possible. It's 120 miles from Avery to Troy, even by the most direct route. No one could do that in a day, and especially not under the conditions like they've had around Wallace.

Are you aware that the newspaper accounts place Thaddeus Roe in Avery until the 23rd?

Yeah? Well, I think I've told you what I think about them newspaper reports.

Yes, sir. Can you tell me what Mr. Roe told you about what transpired in Avery on or about August 22nd of last year?

Well, Tad had been under arrest. The Deputy there had gotten the idea that he—

Mr. Redeye, I'm sorry to interrupt, but if you could please confine your response to information regarding the events of the 22nd, the time period following Mr. Roe's arrest. The reasons for Mr. Roe's incarceration are not our concern at present.

Incarceration. That's a four-bit word, ain't it? I think a one- or two-bit word would do well enough.

Mr. Redeye.

Okay, so we're not going to go into all that speculation.

Mr. Redeye—

Right, right. I thought you were interested in speculation. Okay. So Tad's… incarcerated. Sometime after midnight that night, this fella with the keys to where Tad's locked up—I think he said it was a bank vault, or some such—comes and lets him out. The town's in danger of burning down, and it seems they need his help to fight it. Everyone's gone and run off except a handful of the townspeople, and they need help setting a backfire to save the town.

Who was it that let Mr. Roe out?

I don't know that. The way Tad told it, it was just some fella with the keys. Because you don't get out of a locked up place without the keys, you know, by yourself. Leastwise, not outside the Bible. That thing with Saint Peter didn't happen here.

Are you sure he didn't mention a Deputy letting him out?

Yeah, I'm pretty sure. I think I would have taken note of that. But I don't remember him saying anything that would make me think it wasn't a Deputy, neither, necessarily. Might have been. Might not have been.

And who was in charge of this backfiring operation?

Tad was.

What about the Infantry, or a Ranger or a Deputy?

No, it was Tad. There wasn't nobody left but Tad and the townsfolk.

All right. Go on.

Well, so Tad comes out and sees what's going on. The fires were getting very close to town, sure enough, and Tad could see how the men were getting pretty concerned. There'd been some preparations for backfiring already under way, but it wasn't nearly well organized enough, or even in the right place. With the way the fire had shifted, Tad could see that they were going to need a much bigger blaze, and in a different place. So he sets about getting the men organized to getting it done. This is sometime early morning, but still during the night, you know. It's dark.

And what happened?

Well, it worked, of course. No speculation. You don't have to trust the papers for that part of the story. Avery is still there, ain't it?

And then what happened?

Well, as near as I can figure, which sometimes ain't very near, Tad and the other gents are all laying around, praying, crying and what have you. Some time passes, but not much is going on because everyone's so wrung out, don't you know. And lo and behold, here comes a train up the tracks.

From which direction?

Well, hell, I don't know. I don't know that Tad said.

Well, where was the train from?

It's from Avery.

You said that the train came into Avery.

Sure I did. I know what I said. It came from Avery, too.

A train from Avery, coming back into Avery.

That's right.

And who was on the train? Did Roe say?

Yep. The train had them colored troops on it, and the Deputies, too. They'd taken the train out the night before, trying to escape from Avery. They'd busted through one fire, I guess, then had spent most of the night jockeying back and forth between two different blazes. They finally worked their way back toward Avery, I guess, when they'd seen the flames on up toward Avery die down just before dawn.

And the Ranger was on the train, too?

Well, I suppose so. Now that you mention it, I'm not sure he came in on the train. But he showed up about then, too.

Are you are sure?

Well, he must have. Tad didn't say nothing about him being around during the night, but he was there sure enough when the colored boys and the Deputies come back.

How do you know?

Well, that's when they had a little get together about what to do with Tad. They were somewhat put out, don't you know, to find him lounging around in the street instead of locked up in the bank. So they hash some things around and finally decide that they need to put a crew together to go look for the lost men on Setser Creek. So the Ranger and one of the Deputies puts this crew together, made up of some of them colored troops and a few of the crew that'd been on Setser the day before.

Where did they come from?

What, the colored troops? They were on the train, I said.

No, I'm sorry. The fire crew.

Oh. A lot of them had been on the train, too. Apparently all of them weren't, I don't know why.

You said only one of the Deputies went with the crew up to Setser Creek?

Yep. The other one stayed in Avery with the troops' Captain or whatever he was to set things in order there.

Do you know which was which?

You mean the Deputies?

Yes.

No.

So it was the Ranger, a Deputy, some colored troops and some white men that went back up to Setser with Roe?

Well, what am I? White folks or colored folks?

I'm sorry?

I'm a breed. Am I white folks to you, or colored folks?

Mr. Redeye, my opinion—

Look here, I don't care, Mister Slaughter. What you think of me don't change the color of my skin, my name or who I am. I'm just trying to understand your question. Because as I understand the terms, there were more colored folks in that crew than just the troops. There were probably some breeds, like me, maybe even some Chinamen—and I know for sure there were Italians. Do you consider them colored?

Well, just let me clarify that there were some other men in addition to Roe, the troops, the Deputy and the Ranger. Is that right?

Yes, that's right.

So what did they do then?

Well, they went back on down the tracks.

Was Roe handcuffed, or restrained in any way?

No, I don't think so. They had a lot of tool work to do, clearing their way back into where the men were found.

When you saw Mr. Roe, was he wearing a gun?

Yes, he had his Colt on him.

Are you sure it was his own gun?

Yes, it was his papa's Colt he had with him, and the gun leather, too.

Did he say that it was his?

No, I don't think so. But I could tell it was Ash's rig. It was pretty old-fashioned, and well worn.

What's the significance of that?

Well, you know most cowpokes are pretty particular about their rigging. They like their boots and their gun leather custom made. A good pair of boots may last a long number of years, but styles in gun belts and chaps have changed quite a lot in recent times. And most of them boys like to keep up to date, though the greater number not in quite so pretty a way as some do over Washington and Oregon way. Particularly up there in the Okanogan. You ever see some of them boys in their hairy leggings? So I knew Ash's gunbelt when I seen it, and I'm pretty sure I could spot Ash's Colt anywhere, too—not that there's anything very remarkable about it. It's an 1873 model Peacemaker, the one they sometimes call the Frontier Model, just like any other. But I still think I'd recognize it, and be able to pick it out from a dozen others.

Did Mr. Roe mention how he'd come to be in possession of it?

Well, it was Ash's, you know. When they boxed up old Ash in Libby, Tad got the Colt.

No, I mean, did Roe explain how he came to be in possession of the gun when you saw him? Had he mentioned it being taken away when he was arrested?

Well, now, I suppose he must have had it taken away. Wouldn't make no sense to go locking up a man with a gun, now would it? Huh. No, Tad didn't say nothing about the Colt, and how he come to have it.

And what happened then, when they went on down the tracks?

Well, they got down to the gulch there at Setser and had to begin cutting their way up the gulch. From what Tad says, that was a lot of work. Everything was burnt—everything—and logs were down everywhere. You know, kind of like some giant just kind of took his big old hand and just kind of squashed everything flat, in big swipes of his arm. And things were still smoking, of course. Darn hot, real dangerous. Good odds of things flaring up again, too, because although everything was burnt, everything was dry, too. Just because something's burnt over once, especially in a flash fire, it don't mean it won't flare up again, and this time just burn slow and hot. So they were moving slow, and being careful.

I don't think there's a lot to add about what they found up there. The papers have pretty much got that right. Tad's men were sure enough burnt to a crisp, and pretty unrecognizable. The men from the fire fighting crew pretty much cleared trail and acted as scouts, while the colored troops did the hard work—the digging, the sacking, the tagging and the burying. I do think Tad mentioned that quite a few of them were identifiable, though—not just the one or two the newspapers mentioned.

What about the dog?

What about the dog?

Was that true, about the dog—burying it, playing Taps?

Well, Tad did mention them finding a dog there. He didn't say much more about that. But I did notice that the Times piece called the dog both a terrier and a bulldog. It couldn't have been both, so I'm not sure which it was, and Tad didn't say. Another account I heard said the dog was one of the other men's, not Tad's.

Of course, I haven't heard any other account that even refers to Tad. Some accounts say it was some Ranger who was in charge at Setser, and others say it was one of the Deputies. The Times is the only one that gives credit where credit is due—to Thaddeus Roe, you know, or the hero they call Thaddeus Roe.

Which account do you believe?

Well, hell, I believe Tad's. He was there, weren't he?

Where the hell were these other boys? The closest they ever come to a burning tree is a hot pencil.

Did Mr. Roe have anything else to add about the recovery of the bodies at Setser Creek?

Nope. He just said they buried the bodies, and then he left.

He left?

Yep. He left.

With whom did he leave?

I don't know. No one, I think. He just said he left.

And went where, back to Avery? To Seattle?

No, he left. Left them parts and came up here.

What about the Deputy Sheriff and the Ranger?

What about them?

Where were they? Where were the troops?

I don't know. Why don't you ask them?

Mr. Redeye—

No, I'm serious. They all ain't dead, are they? What are you asking me for? Ask them where the hell they were.

Mr. Redeye, I can assure you that you're not the only man we have been interviewing. Please just answer my questions.

You ain't asked me a question there I can answer.

Mr. Merckx: Objection.

Hey now, what the hell is that? I didn't even ask a question. He can't object to me, can he? Much less a straight-out statement. What the—

Mr. Redeye—Mr. Redeye! Hold on now. I'm sorry.

Ha.

Mr. Merckx, I think, was somewhat belatedly objecting to the form of my question. Isn't that so, Mr. Merckx?

Mr. Merckx: Eh... yes. Mr. Redeye, please allow Mister Slaughter to rephrase his question.

I didn't hear no question.

Mr. Redeye—Did Mr. Roe specify any details about how it came to be that he left the vicinity of Setser Creek?

No, he did not. He just said he left.

Did he say anything about having escaped?

Well, no. I didn't get the impression from Tad that he particularly had to escape. It was more like he just left.

Mr. Redeye—how could it be that a man under arrest would come into the possession of his firearms, and then leave, without having had to escape?

Well, that is a pretty good question, isn't it? Sounds like one for the Deputy, to me. Tad just left, that's all.

And where did he say he went from there?

Up the trail to a wagon road into Wallace. He went in through that country where I hear the one fella went crazy and shot himself, and then on down into that stretch where those other fellas hid in the Nicholson Adit—you know, Pulaski's crew.

Roe did not go back into Avery?

No sir.

Not to get his things?

Well, I don't reckon he had no things to get. What

he had on him was what he had. No, wait—he did say he'd gotten some different Levis and boots that morning. And his coat was pretty much done for, too. But that was before they went off to Setser, I'm pretty sure.

When you say "what he had on him," what do you mean?

Well, what the hell do you think I mean? You know, his rig. Ankle express gear.

Ankle express?

On the hoof. Walking duds. Roe's a cowboy, don't you know, so he looked pretty funny in them duds. He set out from Avery walking, not riding. Caulked boots, I think they were, wood-head's stuff.

Wood-head?

Lumber jacks, you know. He had a Stetson on, though, a good one—Cody model, I think. One of them built-ins for a jacket, Levis for jeans, caulked boots, gun-leather. A canteen, I think. That was about it.

Are you certain he didn't board a train for Seattle?

Well, he sure enough would have had to wait around for some time in Avery before that could have happened. The first train from there didn't go out until the next day—the 23rd, from what I hear. So I don't see how he could have gotten down to Heron with a stop over in Seattle. That just don't make no sense.

What about from Wallace? What did he do when he reached there?

Well, now, you should know that took some doing. Dang near half of Wallace burnt to the ground. That fire that came into Wallace was one of the worst. I think that whole section between Setser and Wallace had burnt off, the way Tad described it. It's steep country in the first place, and it don't help none being even on a wagon road when it's been burnt off. Trees were down everywhere, and every last one of them smoking and smoldering. Every so often, Tad would have to stop, and let them caulks in the bottom of his boots cool off, they'd get so hot with him clambering over them burnt trees.

When he finally got down within sight of Wallace, he really had to start taking things easy. There hadn't been anybody wandering around up at the top of the Wallace trail, but down lower there had begun to be plenty of search parties out and such. Tad wasn't any too anxious to run into none of them.

Why not?

Well, see now, he didn't know yet that he was being made out to be some big hero and all. It was still just the evening of the 22nd, and word hadn't even yet got out about what happened in Avery. That article in the Times wouldn't run until the 28th. Tad never did know that he was being called a hero.

So what did he think about what was going to happen to him?

Well, on that day, probably the biggest concern on his part was being arrested again. There was as much talk, apparently, as there had been some days previously about those no-good fellas down on the Gospel, because by now they'd figured out who those men were—well, at least, what they'd been up to. So it weren't Tad's fault, you see. But those four missing soldiers hadn't turned up yet.

To which missing soldiers are you referring?

The ones sent out from Avery on the 20th to arrest him. The ones Tad was arrested for killing.

Mr. Merckx: Objection.

Right, right. You don't want to hear about what happened before Tad was arrested. Just thought I'd try to sneak that in there.

Please go on.

Well, those buffalo soldiers finally straggled in sometime on the 23rd, I hear, but Tad didn't know that. Neither had Charlie Dennis heard that. As far Tad knew, he'd best be sticking to the willows.

Why the willows?

Why the willows... You know, keeping his belly in the brush. Keeping a low profile lest he prematurely find himself making the big jump.

So Mr. Roe still believed he was considered a fugitive?

Yeah, I should say so.

Even though he'd just walked away from Avery, no need for escape.

Yep. And he was right, you know. He was still considered a fugitive, as you say, in Charlie Dennis's mind. So he was right. And so he took his time picking his way around Wallace under cover of darkness that night. That much I do know. When light came on he was down in the Jackass Prairie somewhat.

And where is that?

You know, on the South Fork of the Coeur d'Alene, west of Wallace. I don't for sure what's there now, in the way of towns and such, but long about Evolution. Thereabouts.

Thank you Mr. Redeye. Now—

Hold on there, just one second or so. You want to know if Tad had time to get into Seattle, right?

Well, yes, that was a question.

Well, then, just listen a bit more because this is important. I don't see how Tad could have gotten to a running train any earlier than the morning of the 23rd, and that would have been right there on the South Fork. Now, that being the case, that would have been one train to Spokane, a change to a new line to Seattle—then at least two more trains back to Heron. I don't think that would even be possible, would it? And even less likely on the 23rd day of August this year. I don't think he even would have made it here by train if he hadn't diverted to Seattle.

So how did he make it from Wallace to Heron?

Well, in the old days, when I first come to these parts, there was a good, solid supply line leaving the Mullan Road at Evolution, going from there up to Eagle City via Beaver Creek and Pritchard. The road then went on up over the Bitterroots and into Heron on the Clark Fork. That was how supplies went into and out of the whole Coeur d'Alene mining district in those days. They was packed in either from the Mullan Road—and that bit they called the Jackass Trail, for good reason—or from up the Clark Fork.

Now since then, a whole passel of other trails and roads and rail grades have been put in through there—you know, to places like Delta, Gem, Burke, Union, Myrtle, Raven and Murray. It ain't like the St. Joe valley at all. Probably one of the reasons they was able to stop most of them towns from burning. Good roads, good access, natural fire breaks. Mostly stripped bare of timber, too. No logging for a good long time.

So it weren't too much trouble for Tad to pick a safe path through that country. He didn't say too much about the particular route he took. Only that he went up from Jackass Prairie into Eagle City—the Jackass Trail, more or less. And said he felt enough like a jackass, too. No cowboy likes to be afoot. It's the lowest thing on earth for a saddle bum.

Now, that's a good piece from Evolution up to Eagle—probably 20 miles of hard—though plain—trail, and another 35 from there on up to Heron, and the most difficult part, to boot. So it was lucky he didn't wind up hoofing it all the way. Somewhere in the hills there above Evolution, he comes upon a beautiful bay mare, rig and all, trailing her reins in the dust. Throwed her rider somewhere, probably, in one of the fires. Just ducked her head and stepped out from under. So Tad picks up this mare, brushes her down and tends the nicks she's got on her from embers. No one shows up to claim the mare, so he takes her.

Now this is important because Tad was aware of this problem with him and horses. He told me and Charlie Dennis that—if anyone should ask—that the mare he picked up is at my place. Just so you know, too. No one's claimed that mare. I gave him a fresh mount.

Why should he care about horses, Mr. Redeye?

He's a cowman, Mister Slaughter. And the parts he come from is still cattle country. There ain't nothing worse in these parts than being thought a horse thief.

Well, I'm not so concerned about Mr. Roe and horses.

You may not be, but I can bet some other folks are. And since this is going to get around, as you say, I just thought I'd mention that. And as he'd been going along, trudging along through that burnt out hell of a landscape, he'd sure enough been wishing he had a horse—and thinking about what he'd do to get one. And it struck him that some folks might already think him a horse thief. He'd borrowed one down on the Gospel, one that he later lost in a fire—a roan, I think it was he said—and then he'd mistakenly taken another one from those colored fellas. Now, that one he'd returned, but he didn't think he'd be getting too much credit for it. After this third one turned up, he wasn't too comfortable about his situation with horses.

I see.

Worried, you know, about getting invited to a neck-stretching, with him being the guest of honor. So that's how he come into Heron. By foot and by horse, via Eagle City. And he got there—got to Heron—on the night of the 23rd. Would had to have, you know, to get up here by the morning of the 24th. So I'm satisfied that Tad came up here direct from Avery, and didn't ever get outside Idaho 'til dropping down into Heron from the Bitterroots.

Well, that leads us to the next question, Mr. Redeye.

What's that?

Why is it that Mr. Roe came up to the Kootenai?

Well, now, me and Charlie spoke to Tad about that at length. Which was pretty much like barking at a knot.

Like what?

Barking at a knot. You can a lead a horse to water, but you can't make him drink, don't you know.

Can you explain that further, please?

Well, you see, horses is real easy to lead, you know, because they get well broke with a bit, and—

No, I mean about Tad's reason for coming north.

Oh. Well, old Tad knew well enough why he was back in these parts. But a man's business is often his own, and he'll keep his cards close to his vest, so to speak. Now, Charlie, he'd heard the word that Three Card Monte was headed to the Kootenai for revenge, just like everybody else, so he pressed Tad some.

And what did Mr. Roe say?

Well, look here. Let me give you some background to this. It was long about June or July, I guess, when word got up this way that Three Card was headed north. Well, this got Mr. Thomas Fewkes a bit nervous.

And can you tell me about Mr. Fewkes?

Sure I can.

Will you tell me about Mr. Fewkes?

Sure.

Mr. Redeye—

Hold on just one minute, son. I'm thinking. Look, here's the thing about Thomas Fewkes. He and his brothers were sure enough bad men. There's no denying that. But I'm not so sure that's saying much.

Can you explain that, please?

Well, see, this is how things were. When the Coeur d'Alenes were opened up for mining, the whole area was a pretty rough place. And that's not unusual. Was Tombstone a tough place? Was Deadwood a tough place? Was Virginia City? Abilene? How about the Yukon, or Sutter's Mill? Sure. And the Coeur d'Alenes weren't no different.

Now, some folks might have thought things should be different. You know, the country being so civilized and such. Good, calm country folk populating things up from the west, and all the way across the plains, too. But in the 1890s, the Idaho panhandle was still a place between places. It was still the frontier. Now, the coming of the rails started to change all that, as it will. But things often get worse before they get better, and, you know, there still weren't no law outside the few towns that chose to get themselves some.

So where you had range wars in Wyoming, we had our own thing going here. It was the unions versus the mine owners. Each side was trying to be the law in its own right. And you know, there was a lot of right on both sides. A lot of folks weren't too happy about it any way you cut it, and others, like Wild Bill and the Fewkeses… Well, they ended up on opposite sides of things. It don't mean neither was wrong, nor right, I suppose.

Now me, I'm an outsider to all this. I was a sometime prospector myself, sure, and that's how I first come to the country. But I soon was an outsider to the business. And, well, others like Bill—he found that he couldn't stay on the outside, and neither could the Fewkeses.

Bill Montgomery, he was a pretty independent cuss, and didn't cotton none to the idea of unions. Not at all. He believed that a man should earn his pay, straight up, and if he didn't like his pay he could find work elsewhere. I think he fancied himself, someday, hitting his own streak of paydirt, and owning his own works on his own claim—and he didn't want no one telling him what he'd have to pay, since he knew the work and knew what was fair. He figured he was square enough, and didn't need the law telling him what was fair and what wasn't, much less a bunch of other fellows.

Now the Fewkeses—well, they hung together and they looked out for each other. And, yes, they were a bit of a rough bunch. I don't think anyone at all doubts that they were behind a lot of the trouble in '92, and maybe again in '99. But that's all a lot of water gone under the bridge, and it's wrong for folks to keep harping on it.

And why is that, Mr. Redeye?

Well, you know, Matthew and Steven paid for their

part. Sometime around the crash in '93, they hooked up with a real bona fide outlaw and went down into Nevada stirring up trouble, then came up into the Okanogan doing the same. Their trouble found them out, like the good book says, sure enough, and they were hung. Thomas was sent up for five years for aiding and abetting, I think—he was living over in Washington at that time, and they actually had law on their side there in those years—so they all did their time, you know, in their own way.

So Thomas eventually winds up back in this country, and he's a much tamer man by then—older, and more broken down. He laid so low a lot of folks even said he was dead. But you know, a man lays pretty low when he gets a family and an honest-to-God business. Like Jesse James, you know. Thomas is a respectable man in Libby, or least-wise he was.

And I think the unions had some legitimate beefs in '99. Things weren't nearly what they was in '92, neither, in terms of violence. You know, they called out the militia and regulars in that first one, don't you? So there was some destruction in '99, sure, but it wasn't the general insurrection of '92. Sure, it did lead to some honest-to-God lawless violence later on. But then, you know all about that, don't you boys?

Please go on, Mr. Redeye.

So Thomas hasn't been hiding from the truth or nothing, you know. He's on the up and up, and plays his cards straight. And Thomas is naturally a bit disturbed when he hears old Three Card's heading up this way. Because he sure enough did kill old Ash back in '92, and the Fewkes boys sure enough did burn his place, accidentally killing his wife. And I've sure enough seen Thomas on the anxious seat at the tent meetings over the years, hearing all that about hellfire and brimstone, and thinking someday he's going to get his.

I run into him one day this summer down in Troy—July I think it was—and he's got a look in his eyes you don't want to see on a man. But that's a look we seen enough in men's eyes last August, I can tell you. You know—that look a man gets when he thinks he ain't got long to live, and wants to make peace with himself, and maybe when he's been to church too much.

"Do me a favor, will you, Jaydub?" he says. Now the hide on this steer's getting pretty tough by this time—you know, he's pretty long in horn and tooth—and it's a sorry thing to see a man his age in fear. So I look at him pretty sympathetic, you know. "Keep an eye out for me, will you?" he says. "He's coming, Jaydub, he's coming. He is like a refiner's fire and a fuller's soap. Who shall stand when he appeareth?"

He said that literally?

Oh yeah.

How do you remember?

Well, it's straight from the good book, ain't it? Not too hard to remember that.

And why was Mr. Fewkes so worried? Was it just the legend of Three Card Monte?

Mr. Merckx: Objection.

No, it weren't. See now, Thomas himself was pretty handy with a six-gun, and had often been notorious in these parts for that. In Libby, in the old days, before Tad left these parts, Thomas was well aware of the boy, and of his prowess with a pistol. He'd seen Tad shoot. And what with himself just plain old getting slower and more domesticated, and what with Tad getting to be older and—well, you know—a man, he figured he was going to have his hands full.

And this is where things get complicated. Because you know, it ain't just the old Fewkes bunch no more. Thomas has got his girls, and his girls—except the one—have got their men. And the men folk, you know, even Thomas—well, they've got friends, too, don't you know. And with Thomas being as scared as he was, well, they're all scared. Everyone's got their eyes out—and they are out, if you know what I mean.

So did you convey this information to Mr. Roe? Did you warn him?

Well, now, I don't know that I'd say we warned old Tad of a thing. First off, it was just good to see the boy. Well, hell… the boy? He weren't a boy no more, he was a man, and looked older than his years, I can tell you. I don't know if there's a lot of folks in these parts who could have recognized him.

And why is that?

It was more than just age. The things he been through down there in Avery—hell, that would age anyone, wouldn't it? He looked like hell itself—burns, dirt. Some damn cross between a devil, a cow man and a lumberjack he looked. Damn sorry sight. Pardon me, ma'am.

Was there any trouble when he arrived?

Trouble? I don't get you.

Was Roe belligerent? Did he threaten Mr. Dennis?

Well, you know, he was wary, sure enough. But threaten Charlie? Hell no. Tad was a good man, and so's Charlie.

Tad comes in while we're having a late breakfast, you see, just having come down from the Yaak. And it's sure enough a scene from one of Buntline's books, I expect. The door comes flying open—and before we even hear it, practically, there's Tad standing with his hand to his Colt, back to the door. He's sweating, and grimy, and looking desperate enough, that's sure.

"I'm Three Card Monte," he says. "That's what they call me. I don't deny it. But I ain't done the things they said I've done."

Well, now, Charlie, he's a level-headed fella, and he just sits there, of course. We both know you don't make a move for a gun if you're not real sure you want to be using it. Tad's got his hand to his shooting iron, sure, but he's not moving nor nothing. Just tense. I don't recall that me nor Charlie says nothing.

"Jaydub Redeye," says Tad, "I know you."

"Sure," I says, "and I sure as hell know you, Tad. You do look rougher for the wear, though, sure enough. Been rode hard and put away wet once too often."

"I reckon," says Tad. "Who's the Foresty man?"

Well, Charlie's an oak post, sure enough, and able to speak for himself. He tells Tad who he is, and tells Tad to calm down. "I'm not the law in these parts," he says, "I'm just a Ranger. This is Montana, Tad, so just relax." By this he meant, you know, that Tad weren't in the pan-handle no more.

"The word's out on me, ain't it?" Tad asks. Well, sure enough it is. And Charlie tells him so.

"And I think you ought to go into Troy, Tad. It'd be good to turn yourself in. Frontier justice is a thing of the past on the Bull."

Well, that was a good line of Charlie's, sure enough. But it was a bit of wishful thinking, as events would prove. Still, it seemed to do the trick with Tad. Still wary, he kicked the door shut—well, I don't want that to sound more dramatic than it was. I'm no pulp writer. He shut the door with his foot. And he did go to the windows of

Charlie's cabin to take another look around outside before settling in. Charlie offered him some grub, which Tad was plainly glad to get. He sits, and sets to with a vengeance. On the grub I mean. Hey, there, Mister Merckx, can I object to myself?

It's all right, Mr. Redeye. Just say what you want to say. Your corrections go in the record, too.

That's the right way of handling it, I suppose. Sure. Well, so, in all fairness to Tad, Charlie goes to telling him what the lay of the land is around Troy and Libby. Thomas Fewkes, I don't think I mentioned, has a place down there in Libby. His wife passed a few years ago, and he lives with his youngest daughter. And he'd been sticking pretty close to home, because of the fires, helping with work down there on the fires. You know, they diverted Flower Creek down there, to water the South side of town, and that's a lot of work. Most of the law was up on either the Yaak, or still up in the Pipe Creek drainage. The fire did a lot of damage here, too, you know. Sylvanite was a total loss. Burnt to the ground.

Well, so, Charlie fills him in on all this, and lets him know that a whole passel of folks is pretty edgy about him showing up on our stoop. And again he encourages Tad to ride into Troy and give himself up.

"I can't do that," says Tad.

"Why not?" old Charlie asks. "You got something better to do?"

"That's my business, I reckon," Tad says.

Charlie's starting to get a bit itchy at this point. The conversation seems to be going in circles, cutting a big loop, and still coming out nowhere. "Well, that may be your business. And you've a right to your business. But other folks have a right to their own, too, Tad. Where do those rights come together? Where do they meet? Where do their rights end and yours begin?"

Well, it's a good thing Tad's a reasonable man. This talk of Charlie's would have rubbed a whole lot men backwards up their spine. "Folks have got their rights, that's true," says Tad. "But I don't see where theirs runs up against mine. I ain't hurting no one."

Charlie points out to Tad that he's got a reputation, and that he's got to work some to overcome it. Until he does, folks have a right to mistrust him. It's natural. Now, it ain't right, Charlie agrees, that someone can get a reputation they don't deserve. But milk don't deserve to get spilt, neither, and it's only most folks who are above lapping it up off the floor. "Are you most folks, Tad," Charlie says, "or are you better than that? Are you too proud to lick the floor when it's called for? I've been hungry enough at times to know I would, if I needed to. What about you? What do you hunger for? Stop wasting my time."

Well, this gets Tad's attention. He grants Charlie's point, but then presses it on others. Why, he wants to know, does this apply to him and not to others?

"What, you mean Fewkes?" says Charlie.

I jump in here. I point out to Tad that Thomas has done his part. He's lived down his reputation, and he's done his share for folks around here. He hasn't been too proud. No one's cut him a big chaw, and he hasn't asked for one.

Well, this didn't seem to make much of an impression on Tad. We find out why, of course, soon enough, though Tad don't tell us right off. So Charlie kept on pushing.

"Look, Tad. Revenge isn't going to get you anywhere." He looks Tad square in the eye, and I think he was truly serious when he says it. "You want to kill somebody, Tad, kill me. Let's put an end to it. Right here."

Well, at this, Tad eases back in his chair. He gets this real far-away look in his eyes and leans back. The chair goes up on two legs, he puts his fork down, takes off his Stetson and runs his hands through his hair. He looks out over to the window.

"Kill me," he says, real softly, and repeats himself. "Kill me."

What the hell, I think. This fella ain't no killer.

He stands up quick and pulls out his Colt. It happens so fast that neither Charlie nor I know what the hell is happening, and I dang near shat myself. I reckon Charlie did, too. But Tad just plunks that Colt down on the table, so hard it bounces twice. He mutters something about going back to the Gospel and heads out the porch.

Charlie and I don't really know exactly what's happened. Through the open door, we can see that Tad's horse is still tethered there, and it don't sound as if Tad's moving off anywhere on foot. So we just sit for a few minutes, looking at each other.

Soon enough I get up and head outside. Tad's just sitting off the edge of the porch with his head in his hands, and I go and sit beside him. Charlie follows with Tad's hat, and his Colt. He stops in the doorway.

"A lot of men have died because of me, Jaydub," Tad says.

Now, I'm thinking—oh my God, then it's true. Them stories that folks tell. He's talking, of course, about what's happened since he left the Gospel—about the fella he winged, the one who later died, the soldiers he thinks are dead, and about those poor fellas on Setser Creek.

Did he tell you that, or is that your opinion?

No, he told me that. If he hadn't, I'd still be thinking sure enough that I was hearing his confession for the dark deeds of his past. And you know, maybe he had some—in fact, like all of us, I'm sure he did—but killing folks just wasn't one of them.

So why the remorse, if that's what it was? Why remorse, if he wasn't guilty?

He was just sorry those men had died. Is that too hard to believe?

No, no it's not.

You know, a lot of men just feel bad when they get caught. Until then, it don't bother them none at all. But there's another kind of sorrow, as they say: the kind that—

Now, if I could interrupt for a moment. You mentioned the party of men who ambushed Mr. Roe on Slate Creek. Do you know who those men were?

Nope.

Did Mr. Roe speculate about who they were, to your knowledge?

Nope. He didn't talk about them, other than to say he was sorry that one fella he shot later died.

Can you speculate about who they were?

Well, sure I can.

Will you speculate for me?

Well, I'm not so sure I want to. There are some things I don't mind speculating about, like newspaper men, because I don't figure none of them are going to take out after me. But mostly, talking about things you don't know for sure is sometimes a real good way to get somebody in trouble—and the one who gets in trouble just might be me.

Well, Mr. Redeye, I will remind you that you are under oath for this interview, and that the law both binds you to answer my questions, and protects you. The law very clearly distinguishes between first-hand knowledge, hearsay and opinion. I'm merely asking for your opinion, and it will go on record as such.

I'd say it was just a group of hotheads looking for a reputation. You know, like the Fords, or like the fella that shot Hickock in the back. Some toughs with chips on their shoulders who wanted to be known as the ones who got Three Card Monte. It's a good way to earn friends. And enemies, too, of course, sometimes.

Thank you. So, what happened next?

Well, Charlie, he's pretty well convinced, too, that Tad's not much of a danger. He tries to give Tad his Colt back, saying again that he's not the law in these parts, you know, and a man shouldn't be without his sidearm. But Tad ain't taking it. He said he's done being a danger to himself and to others.

"If you're no killer, Tad," Charlie says, "why do you think you could become one? That's not the cloth you're cut from."

Well, Tad looks up at that. "Anyone can become a killer," he says, and I'm pretty sure he's thinking of his papa when he says that. "It just takes a reason."

Well, Charlie comes right back on that one. He kind of surprised me, like it was something he'd spent some time thinking on. "Anyone can leave good reason for bad reason. Anyone can take good news and turn it to ill. I suppose that a man can even lose faith. Really lose it, I mean. But if you know who you are, really know who you are and what you're made to be, that's a lot harder to do."

Tad looks away, and off into the distance. "And what am I, Charlie?"

"We'll see, won't we?" Charlie turned and walked away.

That made Tad mad. Now, I didn't see what Charlie

was driving at here, but I guess Tad sure did. He jumps up and follows Charlie back into the cabin. "What the hell are you getting at, Charlie Dennis?" he yells. "Are you trying to say its wrong for a man to defend himself and his family?"

"I'm saying there's a lot of ways of doing that, Tad. And there's stories older and more tragic than yours. They don't all end in revenge. It's not all Shakespeare and Jonson, you know."

Now, what the hell old Charlie meant by that, I still don't know, but Tad seemed to. "What are the options, then, Charlie?"

"Blessed are the peacemakers, Tad." And Charlie hands him the Colt, speaking about more than cold steel. "For some it ends on a hill. For some it simply means there isn't any pay-back. There is no defense."

Tad got quiet then, and takes the pistol. "Yeah, boots on or no," he says, real sarcastic like, holstering the Colt.

"I'm sorry," comes back Charlie once again. "I didn't know you were looking for the easy way out. I had you confused with someone else."

"It's not revenge," says Tad.

Charlie was finally getting through. I saw now what he was doing. He was just trying to get Tad to fight back some, in order to get at the truth, which for some reason Tad had buried deep. "How's that?"

"It's not revenge," Tad says again. "I didn't come up here for revenge."

I jump in again here. "Everyone knows you said you were going up to the Kootenai to settle a debt, Tad. You did say that, didn't you?"

Tad nodded. But he still didn't say nothing. Just stood there for a bit, then walked back over to the doorway, stretched out his arms and held himself on the frame.

Something clicked with Charlie, I guess. "There's

more than one kind of debt, isn't there, Tad? More than just chits to collect? There's chits to pay, too."

"I used to have some use for the truth," he says. "Maybe I still do."

And then he tells us.

Tells you what?

Oh, hell like you boys don't know. About old man Roe, of course. That's a big part of why we're here, ain't it? I know, I know. You know I know, and you know I know you know. You just want me to go ahead and tell you, anyway, so I will. So this is how it is.

Ash Montgomery settled down in the little strip of bottom land on the north bank of the Kootenai above the falls. This was in the days before the rails come through, and the Kootenai was still hard to get to. But all the good land was taken up in the more accessible areas. You couldn't get nothing within fifty miles of Bozeman by then.

Now, you may not know, but the Kootenai was pretty late in being settled, though it was explored by Thompson in the early part of the last century. Most areas of the "Great American Desert," which is what they used to call the frontier, were first settled either by prospectors, ranchers or rail crews—and the associated hangers-on. But these parts here were mostly settled by homesteaders and lumber barons. Sure, Libby Creek itself was prospected during the war between the states, and there were some placer outfits scattered here and there. But this was forest country, really, and you had to be tough to scrape out a homestead on the Kootenai. The government gave you your one hundred and sixty acres, sure. But if a family could eke out a living well enough to actually stay in residence on a spread for five years, they was doing good. But a lot of folks still proved up, you know.

Proved up—what does that mean?

Well, you know, you actually had to show that you were making improvements on the land, making it work as a homestead. This was to prevent corruption. What a lot of ranchers and timber outfits would do is hire folks, or dupe them into filing homestead claims on important stretches of land. For ranchers, this would typically be parcels with water sources, and for the lumber barons it would be parcels with particularly nice stands of government timber. Now, if they could… uh, persuade… settlers to file claims and sell out cheap or even sign away the timber rights, they could get legal control of the land.

Folks would still have to develop their claim, of course, but the way this would work is this. A man would file a homestead claim, intending from the get-go, most likely, to sell out and move on—doing the same thing again somewhere else. So he would go through the motions—clear a small plot of land, enough for a one-room cabin and a small garden or a corral, maybe some pens. And he wouldn't really live there. He'd come back often enough to make it look more or less lived in, and to keep a some livestock or truck growing. You know, a few goats or hogs, or even a few head of cattle. Something that would more of less care for itself. In the meantime, he'd be mainly occupied with something else, something easier than scraping a living out of the land.

And after keeping this nonsense up for five years, well, the land would be his and he could do with it as he pleased. And what pleased this kind of man the most, of course, was easy money. So he'd sell out to the highest bidder. Sometimes he'd even be advanced money for doing this, and in some extreme cases, he'd in reality have already sold out—though, of course, not in actual title—and the work of proving up would be handled by the real owners, if the parcel was in a place where they could get away with that.

Now, the government was actually pretty generous in these parts, because of the tough winters here. I'm not sure if this was true elsewhere, but around here you'd get five months of the year where you wouldn't have to actually live on the land. You know, you'd be able to absent yourself from the place to earn additional income in some other way. And on most spreads this was a real necessity.

Now, for a real homesteader, the proving up was real work. Because if you intended a donation land claim to be your honest-to-God home, you couldn't go about that by just clearing an acre or two. You'd have to clear dang near the whole of the usable portion of the parcel, whether that was arable land for crops or grazable land for sheep or cattle. And, you know, you'd have to stump farm for a while, since it would take several seasons, in many cases, to actually clear them all out. Especially on the Kootenai. You'd spend whole summers doing that.

Now smarter folks don't need to be told there's easier places to farm than this part of Montana. That's sure enough true. In fact, if it hadn't been for the so-called Indian trouble, I don't know that farmers would ever have paid much attention to this country. But where there's forts, there's a need for truck that don't have to be freighted in. And once enough land is broken to satisfy the needs of the army, of course, production will soon be able to meet the needs of the population in general—settlers, prospectors, ranchers. And because of the remoteness of the area, it's a profitable business. Tough though it is, and with its own good share of risk, prices are high enough to be able to compete easily with goods brought in from the civilized world, don't you know.

Now the thing about this country, the thing that made it work, was the development of dry farming techniques. You'd have to pulverize the top-soil to get started. You couldn't just expect a plow to break up the ground. It's too hard for that because of the extended dry seasons. You'd have to do in-season planting, and let the ground lay fallow during the summer. Good yields would only come from certain crops—hard wheat, oats, barley, and flax. The soil was rich enough to support a small truck garden and some potatoes, for your personal use. And you'd always have to deal with rust and hailstorms, so there was very little guarantee of a harvest. In the early days, too, you'd still have an Indian raid from time to time.

But by the time the iron horse come through down on the Clark Fork, folks had figured out how to get a yield of eighty-five bushels per acre in wheat. That's pretty good for country like this. And the boosters and land speculators managed to convince a lot of folks hungry for good land that dry farming could push the better parcels to one hundred and sixty bushels per acre. You could lose every third crop to hail or rust, they claimed, and still manage to turn a profit on the work.

Now, as long as market prices for wheat were high, I suppose that was true. I first come out this way in that period, just a young fella—not for farming, mind you—and I didn't have to come far. Those that did, though, well, they come cheap. On the Great Northern, they had such a vested interest in seeing this land developed—you know, because they needed freight to haul on their rails, and someone has to produce this freight—well, they'd ship a fella out here from back east for twelve and a half dollars, one way only.

One way ticket, express to nowhere. Because the bottom fell out of the wheat market in '73. And that was that, for a while. When the beef boom took over, well, then a lot of the land went over to ranchers. That's where the Kootenai comes in, because homesteaders who didn't want to deal with ranchers, you know, well, they're looking for someplace a little more out of the way. But then, of course, the bad winter of '86 sort of put the cap on the cattle boom. From there, farmers and ranchers both had to learn from some tough lessons, and things went from easy speculation and boom times, to just settling down to hard work.

And hard work it is. It takes tough people, with a good independent streak—maybe, even, people that don't particularly like other people much, or least-wise can get along without them well enough. And the risks are still there, sure. But what they called the Indian problem's been licked for a good a long time. And of course, the rails guarantee a more steady market, and now you've got irrigation and pest control and such. I'm glad I'm in horse flesh, because the new way of doing things, I'm pretty sure, would be a little too much for me. I'm getting a little snow on my crown, you know, what's left up there—and getting hard to teach new tricks. But I hear tell that millions of acres are being homesteaded every year now.

Yeah, so anyway, here on the Kootenai, once things started getting civilized, it would get harder and harder to prove up on your piece. They'd send government boys out to actually ride herd on land agents, timber cruisers and claim jumpers. It was pretty rough times for a while, and it was not for the faint-hearted. It was almost like range wars in a way. Even into the last few years, Charlie Dennis himself has been shot at, just going in and inspecting land claims.

No one ever had no problems with Bill Montgomery, though. No sir. He first cut his spread, I don't know, probably long about the time of the Centennial. I weren't around here then, so I don't rightly know for sure. But he's got a fair spread, neighbors is sparse, and he likes it that way. It's good that it's a man like Bill who is working it here, and not someone softer.

Bill proves up by working the land three seasons a year. Spring wheat and winter wheat, summer stump ranching. During the snowy part he works as a mine hand down in the Coeur d'Alenes. It's an odd life he's leading, one foot in God's good earth and the other a whole lot deeper, if you get my drift. Not many men could have done it—you know, pretty much livin' like a hermit for nine months and like a devil for three. Wild Bill he was, no doubt, as long as winter lasted.

Well, one winter, long about the time they started bringing placer out of Libby Creek, Bill ups and brings a wife back with him. She's a woman who's sowed her oats, too, just like Bill. But hell, Dunn Creek Nell's their nearest neighbor, so who's to care? Now I never did learn her name, I don't know why. Just called her Missus Montgomery, or Miss Monty. Seemed to work fine by her.

Now Bill's just got a one-room cabin in them days, and it ain't really fit for a wife and a growing boy. The winter of—

Excuse me, Mr. Redeye. A boy?

Oh. Yeah. Well, that's Tad, you know. He come along soon enough after Miss Monty come to the place, if you get my drift.

Thank you.

Yeah. Well, so, the winter of '86, you know, was pretty rough on everyone, and Bill had started staying closer to home winters. After struggling through that one, and after losing their dry goods during the big flood the next year, they decided to build themselves a proper house on a rise at the east end of their place. They finished it about the time that hard-rock mining started in Libby. '89 I think it was. And that's when Ash first ran afoul of the Fewkeses, there in the Libby Creek mines. Because he weren't too keen on spending the winters down in the Coeur d'Alenes, not leaving a wife and boy behind. Libby's the closest town, you know, and there ain't a lot of folks to help if help is needed.

So this all changes when the rails come through. Rail lines change all kinds of things, you know. Libby was a boom town then for a while, sure enough, while the line was being built. And it was wild as any boom town gets. The Fewkeses get more popular, and Wild Bill gets a little less. He was settling down, you see. A wife and boy will do that to a man.

But rails bring some other things with them, too. One of them things is rod-riders—tramps and hoboes, we call them now. And they don't just ride the cars the way them other things ride your union suit, you know. They walk the tracks, too.

So the winter of '91, when the tracks ain't even completed yet, just the grade cut and things still under construction, these two old prospectors are out walking the grade, headed down from Bonner's Ferry. They've been in Troy, but the place wasn't much friendlier in those days to shiftless folk than it is now—maybe less. So these two old boys get run out of town on a rail, literally, and thrown out into the snow. It's January, bitter cold, and the Kootenai's even frozen over most places.

So these two poor old gents are near death, struggling their way down toward Libby. Just about the time the one gets to the point of simply laying down to die, he sees lights in a house on the opposite shore. This would be Wild Bill's place. So this fella decides to brave the ice on the river and try for the house on the knoll.

His partner's having none of it. He ain't doing nearly as poorly, and his backside remembers the rail in Troy a little too well to want to be taking his chances with civilized folk. Then these two boys part company. They've had some years behind them, and it's a sad parting.

Now the wind's screaming like whistling eagles as the old coot makes his way to Ash's place. He's just got a blanket wrapped around his one pair of coveralls, a wool cap, no gear, and naught but rags wrapped around his feet, which are turning blue—gunny sacks, for real, tied up with clothesline. No bull. He knocks at old Bill's place, and when the door is opened he asks for a piece of cornbread.

Now this here tells you something Bill, and even Tad, and the kind of stuff their people is made of. Bill takes that old fella in, feeds him a good hot meal. His wife draws a hot bath for the gent, and while he soaks he smokes a good fresh pipe-full of tobacco. Where he's been, apparently, they ain't got much use for hair on the head, so he's gone and moved it down to his chin. There's a bunch there, and it wags up and down as he chews down the end of his pipe.

The cold hasn't been any too good for the old boy, and he's coming down sick something awful. Bill and his woman do what they can to care for him, but he comes down with a hard fever, and gets a mite delirious. When a man's sick, you know, he'll say things he don't necessarily want others to hear, and wouldn't volunteer even if he were drunk. So they find out some things about the old boy, and stuff he won't never talk about with them again.

The old boy is a sure-enough old timer, a sourdough who'd been out to Sutter's Mill in '49, and when things played out there, he was one of those insane fellows you might have heard about who tried to cut across Death Valley from Bakersfield up to Owyhee. Well, you know how that turned out. So he's one of those boys, you know, the crazy ones who've made and lost more than one fortune, and are pretty content with that way of life—living high while the dust and nuggets is there, and being content when he's down that he'll sure enough be up again since he's been there before.

So somewhere along the way, he's prospected up and down the Kootenai, and with this partner of his, taken some pretty fine galena from a mine they've discovered—

you know, years before, real lost mine stuff. Times being what they are for this gent, they've gotten pretty tough again. And when things have played completely out it seems that the next deck to draw a card from is this here lost mine on the Kootenai. They're on their way to find it again when Troy happens to them.

So who is the old boy, really? They never really find out. He tells them his name is Roe. That's all. No Christian name, just a letter. J. It's not an initial, he says, just a letter. Old man Roe.

But does it matter who he is? Apparently not, not to the Montgomerys. He takes to young Tad like a fresh augur to alder, and it gives old Ash a lot more peace of mind about being gone from the place. Bill's old one-roomer, with its old Sively stove, is still down on the bottom land, and Bill fixes it up right nice for the old boy. So old man Roe settles in as a regular part of the Montgomery spread.

Now, he's a genuine character, that's for sure. In all these years, in all these wild mining camps, old man Roe has picked up his own unique brand of folklore, the kind of thing that makes most fireside stories seem tame. He's the kind of fella, you know, that Service spent plenty of time with up in the Yukon in later years—the kind of fella you could base a whole series of books on, if you was a writer.

He tells Tad all kinds of tall tales as he's growing up.

Am I talking too much?

No, you're doing fine. Go ahead.

All right. Well, you know, he makes Tad red maple whistles that winter, and when the owl hoots he tells Tad that spring has arrived. When the grass comes on, he's got Tad out there looking for fairies among the blades—has Tad convinced that the forest is a jungle and that there's monkeys out there. When a rooster crows, Tad's awhirling and turning like a twisting bronc because the old man's told him that a rock turns over every time a man-chick squawks. And Tad sleeps better at night knowing that the old fellow in the moon is looking after him from above—except for when the coyote howls, because that means a storm is coming, so the old man says.

Then hell breaks loose, of course. It's just a few months later that the house burns, Miss Monty dies, Ash blows into Libby shooting up Billy Blew's, and he takes a fatal slug from Thomas Fewkes' forty-four.

What more is there to tell? Well, just a bit more. But it's the part that answers the why that Charlie Dennis and I had been waiting to hear. When Tad's folks died, you see, old man Roe took Tad in. The new house on Monty's place was gone, sure enough, but the old one-room was still there. And I'll be danged if old man Roe didn't make a go of that spread, with just him and the boy to do it. Turns out he's probably not quite as old as he looks, and he's plenty spry. How he makes a go of it, being short-handed, though, no one's really quite sure. Some folks say that he'd found his lost mine again, and was paying for supplies in gold nuggets. Others said that he'd been drawing on accounts down in San Francisco, while others claimed that old Bill, in his wilder days, had put in quite a store of high-graded ore on the spread.

In any event, old man Roe sets up shop there in the old one-room with Tad, and raises him like his own son. This old boy is an educated fellow, too. He knows books, and buys all sorts of them to teach the boy from. Not just classics, neither, but he's on top of the latest in science and what they call literature. The little cuss is growing up from simple farm hand into the sharpest mind in the valley. Within a few years, little Tad Montgomery has become Thaddeus Roe—to everyone, that is, except the government. Because, you see, old man Roe doesn't exist. He's got no identification, nothing to prove he is who he says he is, and there's no record of any J Roe to be found nowhere. Old man Roe is a man without a past. So Tad can't be formally adopted.

This is why, if you try to dig up anything on Thaddeus Roe, you come up empty—like you and your outfit has, no doubt, Mister Slaughter. Thaddeus Roe doesn't exist. He's a character of legend, just like Three Card Monte, and even Tad Montgomery. Without old codgers like me, you can't prove men like Tad ever walked on two legs.

And what did Tad have to say to you and Mr. Dennis, about old man Roe?

Why, that was the debt he had to pay. That's why he left the Gospel.

What debt, Mr. Redeye?

The debt that one man owes another who's treated him square, Mister Slaughter. Do you know how rare that is?

Old man Roe raised Tad right, a God-fearing boy with respect for his fellow man. He trained that boy up right, sure enough, like the proverb says. And when it was time, and when he thought it was right, he sent him away to stop being a boy and to learn to be a man. Tad dwelt on that a lot, Mister Slaughter. He hadn't forgot it, no sir, and came home to see that the old man didn't spend his final years alone out there on the Kootenai.

It's a simple story. It's too bad it ended so badly.

Were there more words exchanged between you and Mr. Roe while at the Bull River Ranger Station?

Well, now, let me think. I don't think so—least-wise, not much.

What about afterward?

Well, I can tell you about that, sure. Charlie and I felt pretty thick in the brain case about never once thinking that Tad's motives for coming up to the Kootenai could be so simple. We weren't alone on that score, of course—but when we heard the truth, it made sense, and we convinced Tad that others would see it that way too. The ones who counted, anyway.

So this is the plan we put together. We figured the safest place for Tad to be was someplace public. Troy was closest, and seemed as good a town as any for Tad to surrender himself in—better and safer, probably, than Libby. To square all suspicious minds, I stabled the bay that Tad had picked up at my place and gave Tad a fresh mount. Charlie decided that it would be best to drop all talk of Three Card Monte, and that Tad should simply turn himself in as Tadpole Montgomery, his birth name. Yeah, that's right. Don't snicker, son.

Before we leave my place, we give Tad time to get cleaned up. I know he's a cowpuncher with some pride, so I outfit him with some clean flannel, a pair of my brother's old Justins and a good oilskin, since we're expecting rain the next day, at last. Rain which don't come, though. But from my place, Charlie and I ride down into Troy with Tad.

The spot we've picked for the surrender is the hotel saloon. Well, it's really not a saloon, there, at the Doonan. It's what they call a bar. Troy's a pretty dry place, relatively speaking, being more of a sod-buster's town than a busted boom town like Libby. It's a calmer place, and the hotel saloon—the bar—is not like the kind you read about in old five-cent novels. It's right peaceful, and civilized.

You know, when men start shooting each other, it's not really like it might have been in the days of Aaron Burr and Old Hickory. Not that civilized, if you want to call it that. Nor is it quite so colorful as the Old West writers would have it, neither. If you read the novels, the fella who's been wronged, you know, takes the most public opportunity to avenge himself. He'll wait till the varmint who done him wrong walks into a saloon, and then he'll either kick the door open, guns ablaze, or call the man out into the street for a right civilized cow-town duel. Even the black hats do it this way.

In my experience, it don't happen like that. If a man wants to kill another man, he sure enough knows that the other fella's going to be aiming for a killing, too—so he'll do what he can to bushwhack a fella, to lay low and guarantee himself a strike. Rattle on one end, maybe, and bite from another. Now, it's certainly true that Wild Bill Hickock got himself shot in a saloon, and also sure enough true that old Ash went after Fewkes in Billy Blew's. But those were exceptions, not the rule. So Charlie's plan was the right one, sure enough.

As we expect, the Sheriff's still not back from Sylvanite when we ride into Troy, so Charlie wanders off to bring him in. Tad and I get ourselves set up with a bottle, and settle down for what should've been a short wait, with our backs to the wall, as is prudent. Now, I think this is where Charlie and I made a mistake.

How so?

Well, looking back, Charlie should have ridden on into Troy a good couple of hours ahead of us. That way he could have made sure that the proper folks would be there to welcome Tad, so to speak. As it was, Tad was left in the care of possibly the worst fella imaginable. Me. When I get a few drinks in me, my judgment just tends to drift on south.

So we're there about an hour or so, and folks are coming and going from the Doonan Hotel. Tad now looks like a pretty swell dude, and is attracting some attention. I'm pretty sure that some folks were recognizing him, too.

There's not a lot of folks around, of course, because of the fires—but what folks there are is still nervous, and anything out of the ordinary attracts attention.

Tad and I aren't really talking much, having had our tongues pretty well wrung out earlier in the day, and Tad knows he's going to be doing a hell of a lot more talking soon enough. So we're just sitting there, taking it all in. And Tad's getting more and more nervous with each passing minute.

I got to say at this point that Charlie Dennis does deserve an awful lot of credit for bringing Tad into Troy peaceful like. It's not that Tad himself was any threat—a powder keg can't be blamed, you know, if someone who don't know better sets a match to it. Charlie just a had a way of defusing the whole situation, you know, like the way I got with horses. And I—well, I just don't, when it comes to men. I suppose I just made Tad more nervous, because I was plenty nervous myself.

When the saloon clock struck three, well, we'd had just about enough. The waiting was getting to be too much. So we decided to clear out. Now, to get out to Sylvanite, Charlie'd had to take the ferry across the Kootenai there at Troy, then go on up the Yaak. To get back, of course, he'd have to come the same route. "Well, don't it make sense," I says to Tad, "that we could meet them half way?" You know, go on down to the ferry and wait for them on the other side. Tad could get into custody faster that way than if we just waited here, like tramps on the hotel stoop. Besides, we'd probably end up meeting them before we even got across the river.

Tad was sure getting itchy, too, so this proposal sounds good to him. Now, of all things, just when we're getting ready to head out, who should walk into the Doonan Hotel bar but Thomas Fewkes himself?

Now, this little scene was beginning to develop the flavor of one of them tall tale honest-to-God western stories. Because I can tell you that Thomas Fewkes does resemble a figure out of something you might read. He's a striking looking fellow, particularly when you're feeling a mite edgy. He stands an inch or so over six feet, and carries his weight like he's lived well, but not too well, if you know what I mean. He's a got a sharp-looking flat-brimmed low-crowned beaver Stetson that marks him as an old-time Montana man, sure enough, with a nice horse-hair band studded with conchos made from Liberty nickels. He's got a nice split-cowhide coat where most folks up here wear wool or tin, and though he don't ride much no more he's got a mighty fine pair of custom-mades that fit quite natural on a bow-legged old boy like him. His lip whiskers has gone pretty light in shade, you know, and you can tell that droopy thing's been growing there a good long time, and it's seen its share of trail grub passing under it over the years.

So I swallow real hard when I see him come in the door. I can't tell you what Tad was thinking, because I wasn't paying too much attention to Tad right then. I had a real strong urge to vacate the premises, like the handful of other folks must have done right about then. I didn't see none of them skedaddle, but they sure must have—because by the time I got to be able to notice such things again, there weren't no one in the place but me, Tad, Thomas and the drink slinger, who seemed to have gotten a few inches shorter that afternoon.

Well, Thomas, he's a real cool customer, that one. There's no doubt in my mind that he knew what he was going to find at Doonan's. Now, I suppose that someone might have seen Tad ride into the Bull River that morning. And I suppose it's possible that someone might have sent word up to Libby from Troy that Tad had come into town. But I don't think Thomas Fewkes had come down from Libby. I think it must have just been fate that he had happened to be in Troy that day.

Whether he'd seen Tad first himself, or whether one of his cronies had spotted Ash's boy, well, I don't know. But Thomas comes in and I don't suppose he must have even paused before he just comes straight across to where we sat. Now, it seemed like a century or more to me, of course, but I reckon he actually stepped pretty lively. His hands are moving free and easy, I know that for sure, and I suppose he must have been pretty much on edge, but I'm so shaky myself that I can't tell.

I don't even remember rightly what he said when he first walks up. I think he said something to me, you know, just acknowledging my presence. And he nods or something, maybe touches the brim of his hat, in greeting to Tad. But he does ask to join us, and gets the barkeep to bring him another glass. There was still plenty left in our bottle.

Tad's pretty quiet, but seems pretty calm, too. He invites Thomas to sit, which he does, and the two of them commence to talking.

Mr. Redeye?

Yeah.

Mr. Redeye, do you need to take a break of some kind? Ken, can you—

Hey, there. Just hold on, now.

Take your time.

Look, how do you want me to do this?

I'm sorry, Mr. Redeye?

No, I'm sorry Mr. Redeye. Boy am I a sorry coot. Look, I know you want me to tell you what happened there at Doonan's, but I really don't know if I can do it justice.

What do you mean, Mr. Redeye?

Well, I was there, you know. But in a lot of ways it seems like I weren't.

Well, just describe for us what you saw.

If I did that, now, there wouldn't be a lot to tell. I'd just have to tell you that I saw Thomas and Tad just sitting there, talking. Because that's all that happened at Doonan's, mostly. Now, there was a little interesting thing that happened, I suppose. And most of the action was on my part, sorry to say. But I reckon you really want to know what was said.

Yes, Mr. Redeye, we do. Do you remember what was said between Mr. Fewkes and Mr. Roe?

Well, yes, after a manner of speaking. I mean, I remember what they said well enough, and I could give you the impression of it. And even many of the particulars, I guess. But really giving you the words of it would be another thing.

What was your impression, then?

That there was a hell of a lot more being said than what they actually said, if you know what I mean.

Well, why don't you start by telling us what you remember of what they actually said?

I can do that. But I can tell you that my memory on this might not be the best. My underthings was getting pretty frothy, I can tell you, so my brain might have been pretty wet, too.

Just do your best, Mr. Redeye.

Well, that I will. But just be sure that you understand that if you were to ask me another time what they said, it might come out a bit different.

We'll bear that in mind.

All right. Well, this is how it was.

Mr. Redeye—

Yeah. All right. Okay…

So, Tad, he invites Thomas to sit. Which Thomas does. For a minute or two, I suppose, they just sit there and look at each other. They got their hands on the table, but they're not really watching each other's hands, you know—least-wise, it don't seem that they are, though you can bet that's what I'm keeping an eye on. Thomas's hands are gloved, as usual. Tad's ain't, and he does seem a bit conscious of his hands, like they feel naked or something. He's not wringing his hands, really, but seems to want to be covering them up, one with the other, and then the other with the first.

Thomas was the first to speak. "You grown up some, Tad," he says.

Tad takes the bottle and uncorks it. He pours Thomas a drink. "Yes sir, I reckon so."

Thomas downs it. "Why'd you come back, Tad?"

Well, now, Charlie and I had already been through all this with Tad, and I dang near wanted to just blat it out like a branded calf. Unwisely, I guess, I just held my tongue. Seemed wise enough at the time, though.

Well, Tad, he just looks down at the table for a minute, then looks back up at Fewkes. "I guess you got a pretty good idea of that, sir." Doesn't blink or nothing. "And then I guess you don't," he says.

Thomas just gets the slightest bit of a smile. "Well, I don't imagine I'll be seeing your boots up on my porch rail anytime soon, anyhow."

"No, sir, I don't reckon so," Tad says. "We're a little past that, I guess."

Thomas reaches up, which makes me jump a little, you know, and strokes his upper lip. "Well, now, I suppose you are." He pours himself another drink. "I suppose you are, at that. Look here, Tad," he says, and drinks. "There's something you need to know."

Well, Tad, he pours himself another one, too. "No, sir, I don't reckon there is." And he drinks, too.

"Yes, there is, Tad," says Thomas.

"No, sir, there ain't," Tad comes back. At this they go silent again for a bit.

Thomas kind of bites his lip some, and then he starts in. Now, I'll try to tell you as close as I can what he says, but again, if you ask me tomorrow I might get this a bit different.

We understand, Mr. Redeye.

"Well, this is how things are," says Thomas. "What happened to your ma can't be undone. I'm sorry enough for that."

What was Mr. Roe's reaction?

Well, you know, Tad didn't react none to any of this, not that I could tell. He just kind of sat there, not really looking at Thomas. I mean, he was looking at him, but more like he was looking through him. Or like he was looking at someone else. It's kind of hard to explain. If I looked at a man like that while he was talking to me, I'd say that I wasn't really hearing him, you know. That I wasn't listening. I don't know about Tad.

All right. Go on.

Well, Thomas kind of swallows hard. "There are some that haven't forgiven me, Tad, and I don't expect them to," he says. "I don't expect them to. It's something I've got to live with, you know." He paused and looked aside.

"Your pa, now, that's a different matter." He looks back right at Tad. "I can't say I'm much sorry for that, Tad, and that's the truth, sorry to say. Your pa and I were different breeds of men, you know, and that's just the way it was. He didn't care for my kind, and I didn't care for his. That's the truth of the matter. And when we come together, well, we had a tendency to cross horns.

"Now I don't blame him a bit," Thomas goes on, "for coming after me at Billy Blew's. None at all. I was over at Cowell's when I got the word from Matthew about how wrong things had gone with your ma, and I was just glad that you weren't there to see it. And I know how you could hate me for your not being there, and how you might even wish you had been."

Mr. Redeye, what did Mr. Fewkes mean by that?

Well, I think only Thomas could really tell you that. But Tad weren't there on the spread when his mama died, like Thomas says. He was just a kid, you know, and had gone to some kid's party, or something, you know. Thomas's youngest daughter was about the same age. It might have been hers.

Thank you. Go on.

Well, Thomas is pretty serious. "Now if I was your pa," he says, "if I was your pa, you can bet I would have done what he did, too. Accident or no, hell, who gives a damn? Your ma was a good woman and she didn't deserve what happened. No one does. And there ain't no kind of human justice that's going to fix that, now is there?"

I think maybe he expected Tad to say something there, but Tad don't.

"Well," he goes on, "I went on over to Billy Blew's, because it had a good view on down to the ferry then, you know. And I sure enough knew I'd see your pa come hitching up Mineral before long. And I did.

"Now I don't know if you ever heard what happened that day. I got to think you have, you know. But I want you to hear it from me. It's important that you hear if from me. I killed your pa."

He pauses, looking for some kind of reaction from Tad, which he don't get. "I did," he says. "He was gunning for me, and I shot him dead."

He pauses again. "Can I see it, Tad? Do you still carry it?"

Now, this made me real nervous. I can't tell you. It still makes the hair on the back of my neck stand up.

Thomas's hands are still on the table, but Tad's right dips down, and I know he's going for his Colt. I know this, and I know that Thomas knows too, because, damn it, he's asked him to!

Now I figure this is a ruse of some kind on Thomas's part—you know, get Tad to move first. And Tad is falling for it! How in hell Thomas expected to beat Tad in a draw like that, I couldn't figure. But in that split second my mind tells me that there's other look-out men ready to plug Tad as soon as he touches leather, that Thomas knows there's no risk to him. It's a set-up, a bushwhack. The bastard! So honest to God, I head for the floor.

By the time I figure out which side is up, it's all over, you know. All over because there weren't nothing to be over.

Tad just takes out the Colt and sets in on the table. And damn it, Fewkes picks it up! He picks it up… How I lived through that afternoon, I just don't know. I just guess I got a heart like a damn ox or something.

Fewkes picks up the Peacemaker and hefts it in his hand. He's a Smith and Wesson man himself, but he knows the feel of a Colt, sure enough. He hefts it, and spins the barrel.

I don't know how I hear anything at that point, with the blood pounding in my ears. As I struggle back into my chair, I can see the barkeep just poking his head out from behind the bar, too. I ain't the only one hitting the floor, it seems. But Tad and Thomas don't take no notice, I guess.

Thomas sets the Colt back down on the table, careful that the pistol don't point, you know, at anyone. "Yep," he says, "that's the piece, sure enough. You've taken good care of it Tad."

Tad don't take it, just leaves it sitting there on the table. That kind of says something, too, I guess, and he meant it to.

"That's your daddy's sidearm, Tad, and you know he knew how to use it," Thomas goes on. "So you got to know that your pa fired first. He come right into Billy's, pulls up and shoots. I don't got to tell you that he didn't really have no chance. There was plenty of the boys there, and more than one paid for being in the wrong place at the wrong time. But when your pa come up empty, that was pretty much it. And I shot him, and I shot to kill. I'm not sorry I done it. He'd have done the same to me."

Tad just reaches out and kind of lightly touches the Colt at this point, looking down at it. "I suppose, sir," he says, "that you're going to tell me that it's got nothing to do with me."

"No, son," says Thomas, "I ain't going to tell you that."

"That's good," says Tad, "that's good. Because I don't reckon you're shut of me yet." And he looks back up at Thomas, right in the eye. Not mean or nothing, but in the eye.

"No, son, I don't reckon I am," says Thomas.

Tad looks at him hard. "Are you looking for forgiveness, sir?"

Well, at this, Thomas kind of snorts. "Weren't you listening to me?" he asks, and I'm kind of thinking the same thing. "Didn't I just tell you that I'm not sorry about your pa?"

Tad kind of screws up his face at this a little. Maybe the most reaction he has to anything Thomas says. "Being sorry," says Tad, "being sorry or not being sorry ain't the same thing as wanting to be forgiven."

"Hell if it ain't," says Thomas. "Hell if it ain't."

At this, Tad looks at Thomas almost like he's sorry for him, which I can't figure. "Well," he says, "it ain't. And I suppose that pretty much is hell. Because only one of them two things is about you, sir. And the other? Now, that's a question, sure enough."

They fall to silence for a minute. Then Tad straightens up a little. "I got some things to do, sir. But I'll come around, you can bet. You'll see me one last time before we're done."

Thomas pours them both another drink. "Well, now, son, if you're looking for answers, I got one. I sure enough got one."

He and Tad each take a glass in hand. "Yes sir, I reckon you do," Tad says. "And when I figure I'm ready for your answer, you can bet I'll come a-looking."

"That's fair," Thomas says, "that's fair."

Tad and Thomas both drink, and Thomas rises. "Don't think too poorly of me when I'm gone, Tad, if it comes to that—and I suspect it is. I deserve better."

Tad looks down at that. "No sir," he says, "no sir, I don't expect you do. But I don't expect I'll let nothing get in the way of that, neither." And he looks back up.

"No," says Thomas, "no, I don't expect you will." And he turns and leaves.

And that's what there was to it. Tad just watches Thomas's back as he heads out the door, and that was that. Least-wise, that's how I recollect it.

Thank you, Mr. Redeye. I'm sure you did your best.

Damn straight.

Now, Mr. Redeye, how did you read that conversation? I mean, how did the words that they exchanged strike you?

Well, like I think I said, that little talk seemed mighty

peculiar to me—like there was more being said than just the words, you know.

Yes. Can you elaborate, tell me more by what you mean?

Well, it's hard to explain.

Yes, sir, I'm aware of that. But I need you to try, and I don't want to put any words in your mouth on this point.

Yeah, I can see what you're getting at. Well, here's the deal. It seemed to me that a threat was being made. Sure. Now, I'm not sure by who, you know—whether it was Tad threatening, and Fewkes responding, or the other way around. But there sure enough was some kind of challenge being put down. You could feel it. These were steers with a history, locking horns and wanting to put an end to it. And I was pretty clear that the two of them were clear themselves, you know, that an end to things was coming soon. And you know, they weren't going to be waiting for no angels to be cutting the tares from the grain, if you know what I mean. They were figuring on doing the cutting themselves. Finding out who the goats were, and who were the sheep.

But at the same time, there didn't seem to be the kind of bad blood between the two that you might expect from men bent on killing one another. If Thomas were trying to convince me, as I well imagine he has tried to convince others, that he wanted to make peace with Tad—well, the mood of those men on that day certainly did carry something of the feel of folks intent on burying the hatchet, one way or the other, all the same.

Still and all, I came away from Doonan's pretty clear that the hatchet was going to buried in someone's head. There were threats made there, and threats responded to, I have no doubt.

Thank you, Mr. Redeye. But with respect to Mr. Roe, could you be more specific? What kind of threat do you feel Mr.

Roe might have made? What did he say that, to you, constituted a threat?

Well, "Before we're done," Tad says. Those words sure stuck in my mind pretty clear. And, "I'll come a-looking," I remember that, too, pretty sharp. "Nothing will stand in my way." I mean, how many ways can you interpret that? It's as clear as sign language, I'd say. Leastwise, it would be, just to a man listening to the words. And Fewkes talking about after he's gone, and all. I mean, they knew something was brewing, the two of them.

But you look unsure of yourself, Mr. Redeye.

Well, damn it, that's because I am. Because that just don't seem to line up with Tad's brand, you know. There's something there that don't fit, that don't make sense with what happened up at Charlie's, nor out at old man Roe's. And particularly with what happened at Billy Blew's. But there ain't no denying what happened with Tad, neither. No, there ain't.

Yes, sir. Thank you. So, what happened then?

Well, I have to catch my breath, you know. Tad's still looking out the door, and I have to kind of work to get his attention again, and he's pretty silent, but don't seem to be worked up particularly. It still seems good to me, maybe even better now, to go find Charlie and the Sheriff, so we pay off the barkeep, step on over our mounts and ride on down to the Kootenai. It takes a bit for the ferry to come across and get us, and by the time we're on the other side it's about three thirty. We feel pretty naked there on the far bank, and when Tad suggests that we go ahead and ride on up to old man Roe's place, it's sounding like a mighty good idea to me. Tad starts up the trail a bit, and I have a bright idea and ride back to the ferry. It seems a good thing to me to leave word there for Charlie and the Sheriff that we've gone upriver toward Libby.

Well, I think this was a pretty bad mistake.

Why do you say that?

A couple reasons, now. First, I'm pretty sure that Fewkes had guessed wrong where Tad was fixing to go when he said that he had things to do.

What do you mean?

Well, I mean, it would have made sense that Tad would head on up to old man Roe's spread. But when Tad said that, it weren't the plan. The plan was that Tad would surrender to the Sheriff. So when Tad says, "I got some things to do," well, he means giving himself up to the Sheriff. And dealing with Thomas later, no doubt. But Thomas reads this as a reference to the visit that Tad sure enough does pay to old man Roe. So Fewkes does guess wrong, but then he ends up being right.

Because, you see, my bright idea gets Tad out of the Doonan Hotel, and his bright idea puts us up the Kootenai. Now, the really bright thing would have been for me to pipe up and just tell Thomas, back in the Doonan, that we're waiting for the Sheriff. But it don't occur to me. And then, when Tad and I decide to go ahead and ride on up to old man Roe's, it didn't help none to go shooting my mouth off about it to other folks. See, if Thomas had been the only one who knew where we were headed, at that point, it'd be a lot more easy sorting later things out, now wouldn't it? So that's one reason heading on upriver was a mistake.

The other's pretty obvious. The other's the fact that we had a choice there. We should have just headed on up the trail to Sylvanite until we come upon Charlie, one way or the other. Because to other folks, to those who had actually seen us ride in to Troy with Charlie Dennis, it looked pretty much like we was heading away from the law and up toward Libby.

Do you know the ferry operator at Troy?

Well, sure I know him. Bill Dossett.

Did Mr. Dossett recognize Mr. Roe?

Well, I guess you'd have ask Bill that yourself. I don't recall that he let on that he did.

And you didn't mention it yourself?

No sir, I did not.

But you told him you were headed up the Kootenai. What words did you use, exactly?

Well, I says, "Has Charlie Dennis come back this way?"

And Bill says, "No. Least ways I ain't seen him."

So I says, "Well, when old Charlie comes back this way, you send him on up to old man Roe's. Tell him that Jaydub's gone up to old man Roe's."

No mention of Tad Roe?

No sir.

So you don't think Mr. Dossett recognized Mr. Roe?

Like I said, you'd have to ask him. Now, if you're asking whether Bill Dossett spread it around that Three Card Monte was headed up the Kootenai, the answer is, I don't know. It don't have to have had to work that way. I do rather imagine that Bill let it leak that I'd headed up to old man Roe's, and that this other fella was with me. But that's no crime—that's just simple small-town chatter. You don't have to build some conspiracy around such a thing.

Look here, there was plenty of folks by that time that could have been putting two and two together and coming up with a full set of hooves, if you see my point. Too many, really, and that's why we either should have stayed put where we were, at the Doonan Hotel, or headed on up the Yaak.

But we didn't. We didn't. So we headed on up the Kootenai. You been down there to see it?

To see what, Mr. Redeye?

To see the river.

Well, yes, Mr. Redeye. We came in that way, by train from Bonner's Ferry.

Well, then you ain't seen what I'm talking about then, I figure.

What's that?

The Kootenai above Troy.

No, I suppose not.

Well, it's a sight, sure enough. That's a pretty stretch of valley right there above Troy. The view on down river from the south bluff east of town is one of the prettiest in the country, especially long about October, on a clear cold morning. The going through there is pretty easy on both horse and on the eye. Right pretty. Of course, it don't look like much this time of year, what with the snow and all, though that's its own pleasant sight. But the going is nice there in the summer. Much further above Troy, though, on up toward Libby, things get to be pretty tough going—you know, no road to speak of over there. And there's a reason they graded the south bank of the Kootenai along there and not the north.

It's all right on horseback, though of course you have to head on up the bluffs for a good stretch. You can't really stick to the river, particularly in the stretch above the falls. Now, old man Roe's place is above the Falls just a bit, down there in the bottom land that opens up between the Falls and Libby.

And when we come up on the bluff, there above the

Falls, we come up out of the bank of smoke that was still drifting up the river. It weren't thick, you know, but enough to keep things kind of murky. Up on the bluff, though, there was good fresh air, and it was good to be able to see some distance up and down the river. From there, we could see on up into the country where the fires were still burning, but that was some miles away, still to the north and east. So it was pleasant and clear. Rather than dropping back down to the river at the first chance we get, we go ahead and ride up along the bluff until we come above the Roe spread.

This has taken us a few hours, so it's going on seven o'clock by then—not nearly near dark, normally, you know. But once we dropped back down into the drifting smoke, it wasn't really full daylight neither. It wasn't hard to slip on down into to old man Roe's place without being particularly noticed.

So we ride up to the house, right peaceful like. Tad steps off, tethers his horse, and walks on up to the door. He knocks, and turns back to look at me, smiling pretty gently. In a few seconds, the door opens, and there's old man Roe, his head now at about Tad's chest level because Tad ain't a boy no more. And before Tad could even turn back around, well, all hell broke loose. You know what happened then.

Yes, sir. Could you describe for us what happened?

Well now, I was pretty sure you'd want me to. How much detail are you looking for?

Well, Mr. Redeye, as much as you can recall. If you don't mind.

No sir, I don't mind. Not at all. Now, my recollection on this part of things is pretty much clear. We come on old man Roe's place pretty quiet, and a good ride always clears my head some—especially after having done some drinking. So I weren't in anywhere near the kind of fog as I was in Doonan's. No liquor, no sweats, no shakes—no. I was pretty clear when the firing started, and that got me going pretty good. I hear pain can do that to a man—adrenaline, or something.

So the first thing I see, even before I hear shots, is the door frame splintering behind Tad's head, to his right. Two shots, maybe, hitting at almost the same time, though I suppose it could have been one.

The next thing I know, a bullet slams into my horse. I think it must have passed right through, from the left hindquarter and passing out just below the pommel on the right. It was like someone just kind of lifted her up and set her down again, only she decided not to stand. She was a damn fine horse.

So down I go. Now, I see a lot of things from this point, and I'm not sure at all in what order it all happens. Tad reaches behind him, down to his right, and kind of pushes old man Roe back inside, to grab the door and pull it shut. There's already a good splash of blood on the door, I'm not sure whose. Could have been bullets, or splinters flying from the door frame that done it.

Anyhow, my mare, she kind of lifts her head back as her legs cut out from under her, and another slug slams into her head from the left, takes a good chunk out and sprays it around, and I feel the bite of another round in my left thigh. That passes into the mare, too, so now she's taken three shots and is pretty much done.

Tad's mount, on my right, is still standing, so this tells me something as I roll off onto the ground between them. There's at least four fellows doing the shooting, and they're most likely all off to our left, down river. They've been waiting to waylay us in the woods down below Roe's place, most likely, and we've come in behind them by dropping down late from the bluff. They are using Winchesters, sure. And not the newer models, neither. No thirty-thirty—even ought-six. Heavy guns, the forty-fours. No pistols. Distance shooting.

So Tad has got the door shut, and I don't know how he doesn't get hit. With me down, he's the only main target. He steps to his right now, coming up along the porch toward where these fellas are shooting from. He has his Colt out, but he's not firing, you know, and I'm not sure why. I guess because there's no one to shoot at. The other side of the door frame loses a chunk, the left side this time, and I see two or three more shots go in through the door panel.

I know pistols aren't going to be much good in this little spot here. I've got mine out by now, too, and Tad's still stepping down the porch, with shots taking out chunks of the posts beside him as he moves. Still, it don't seem he's being hit. I reach up behind me and pull the rifle from the scabbard on Tad's mount, hollering at Tad to take cover. He don't, of course, and motions for me to throw him the rifle, which I do.

Then we start taking fire from down along the river, too. It's a near cross-fire. The second horse pulls free, but don't make it more than five feet before it's down, shot right through both front shoulders, it looks like. Another bad loss, that one. Took at least one bullet meant for Tad, I think. So this gets me pretty riled. I put a shot into her head just to finish her off.

Lead is flying pretty thick now.

Did you see at any point who was firing upon you?

No. Not once. They were all firing rifles, not one of them closer than a hundred yards, I'd say. The ones down river, over on our left, were behind the stone fence at that end of the place. The ones fronting the cabin, straight toward the river, had the cover of the little rise that the old house used to occupy. So you know, here we have the low ground, and nothing but the cabin and a couple dead or dying horses for cover.

Tad, of course, he's not going for cover anyway. He's got the rifle now, and he's putting it to good use, keeping the heads of those boys over by the stone wall down. So he passes around the left end of the cabin, and out of the line of fire of those boys by the knoll. I see that rifles is sure the best option, so I throw myself over my mare as best I can, and pull my own rifle from the scabbard. As I do this, though, I take this shot here, through my left forearm. It don't hit the bone, I guess, or so they tell me later, but something's messed up bad in there, and I have a devil of a time supporting that rifle.

The cabin gets hit again with another good hail of fire, so I guess that those fellas by the knoll are trying to discourage whatever Tad is up to. Glass flies, and a good chunk of the door just disappears.

I take up position there behind the horse, trusting Tad to cover my flank, and start chucking some lead over that way toward the knoll. I'm kicking up some good dust, but I don't have any illusions about whether I'm hitting anything.

Now there's a bit of a lull in the shooting here. I'm packing Winchester '73s, you know, which is a good thing, so Tad and I can both reload from the forty-four slugs on our belts. And then Tad leaves the cover of the cabin, and the lull is over. He takes off for the fence line behind the cabin, to try to flank these boys over to our left. They're taking shots at him, sure enough, and I can hear that the fence row is taking some pretty heavy damage. This is still just a minute or two into this fiesta. This all happens pretty fast.

I go back to work on the knoll, but the horse proves to be less substantial cover than the fence, I reckon. I've already got a hole in my thigh and forearm, and now take two more slugs. One, here, goes just above my collarbone, and I think I'm done for with a neck wound. The other passes just below, right through the meaty part of my right shoulder. This pretty much puts me out of commission, and I just prepare myself for the worst.

Well, now, the sound of things takes a turn. The volume of fire off to the left drops off a good bit, and I can hear that this bunch of assassins has mounted up and taken off down river. I'm still taking some lead, though, and pretty soon, here comes Tad, moving up quickly to where I'm at, standing tall and squeezing off shots up toward the knoll. The shooting from there stops, too, and things fall pretty quiet. All told, this little thing plays itself out in maybe five minutes.

Without looking down at me, you know, because he's keeping his eyes out for more of these skinks that shot us up, Tad asks me how I'm doing. Actually, he asks me if I'm alive. I tell him, sure, I'm alive.

"Are you hit?" he asks. Well, sure I'm hit, I tell him. How much, he asks, and I tell him. Four shots, that I can tell, and I'm pretty much useless. I do tell him that I think I'll live, and send him off to check on the old man. I haven't seen him since he come to the door, you know, and expect the worst.

So Tad stands there for just a minute, looking around to see if anything looks out of place, you know—making sure that things are safe—and then he heads up onto the porch.

My first concern is about my leg. The bullet don't seem to have passed through an artery or nothing, because the blood ain't pulsing out or gushing, and the slug is apparently still in there. So I tear off a chunk of my shirt, ball it up and wedge it down there inside the left leg of my chaps to keep some pressure on it. I wrap a snug tourniquet around my forearm, and then check out my shoulder. I can run the little finger of my left hand clean through the upper wound, which just kind of leaves a chunk of muscle and skin up there hanging loose. It's bothersome and bleeds, of course, but I'm not too much worried about that. The lower wound's a bit of a problem, though, as I can't really dress it in any way. And it feels like I've lost a bone or two up there. No lung hit, though, I can tell that, and the shoulder blade seems okay.

Well, I get help with that, soon enough. Tad comes back out from the cabin. "The old man's dead," he says, just like that. "The old man's dead."

The first volley, it seems, must have caught him full force. He didn't have a chance. Now, those bullets were meant for Tad, sure enough. I don't think no one set out to kill old man Roe, and it was due to us coming at the cabin the way we did that led to things falling out there that way. We surprised them, I reckon, by coming in behind them the way we did. Surprise has a funny way of escalating things, don't you know.

I'm not excusing the folks that did the shooting, just so you're clear. My stock and me took our own share of lead, too, you know, and it might as well have been me that died as old man Roe. In a lot of ways, I wish it had been me instead of the old man.

"Did you get to talk to him?" I says. Tad just shook his head. Tad had already kind of laid him aside and covered him up, you know, by the time he'd carried me inside. And there was a lot of blood. I mean, a lot of blood. I doubt if the old man even knew what had hit him.

Hell, that was a bad, bad thing that happened there that day. So needless.

Well, Tad fixes me up all right, you know, as well as a fella can do without a doctor. Cleans and dresses the wounds, gets me some coffee and whiskey, and gets some biscuits on. And then he finds a box of shells and starts refilling his gun leather. The rifle had taken every shell from every loop.

"Now look, Jaydub," he says, "I know what you're thinking. And I don't care to hear it."

Well, I didn't figure he did. I mean, we all know that the good book says to turn the other cheek and all, and to love your enemies. But the good book seems to just be made for other times and places, don't it? Who, now, would expect Tad to be any more understanding about old man Roe than his pa was about his ma? Not me.

Expectations aside, I did notice a funny thing there. Tad didn't have to put any shells in the Peacemaker, because he didn't use it there, neither. Just refilled his belt. And under his breath, he says something that I remember very clearly. "Burn the fuel that the fire wants," he says, "before the fire gets there. Then there's no fuel left." I have no idea what he was talking about.

Then he turns to go. "You just relax, now," Tad says. "Charlie should be along any time now, and he'll see you get taken care of. I've got some thinking to do, and I don't reckon bars, shackles and such are going to help me with it."

Well, you know, I wouldn't have blamed Tad for whatever he might have done at that point, so I didn't argue none. I just asked him if there was anything he wanted me to pass along to Charlie Dennis.

"Well," he says, "it's time to put old Three Card to rest, I reckon. Just tell him that."

That was it. And he left.

Do you know where he went from there?

Well, sure he went on into Libby, and into legend, I guess. Crossed the river the next morning at Jack Elliot's ferry. Bill Harmon could tell you about that.

I meant to say, do you know where he went that night after leaving Mr. Roe's place?

No, I don't. He left afoot, of course. And he was limping some. He might have taken a round to his leg. That's all I could tell. I can only guess that he spent the night up in the hills there somewhere.

Charlie and the Sheriff got to the cabin after dark a bit. They took something of a look around, but didn't find no sign of any body there—no sign of anyone else being shot, or nothing. The Sheriff went on into Libby while Charlie stayed there with me. They brought the doctor back there during the night, so Charlie and the doc and I were still there when Tad went down at Billy Blew's the next day.

It was a sad thing to have to hear about, I can tell you.

What do you think happened in Libby, Mr. Redeye?

What do you mean?

Well, most people have assumed that Mr. Roe went there bent on revenge. What do you think?

Well, that would be natural, wouldn't it? Still and all, I suppose that's dependent on the answers to a lot of questions, ain't it? I mean, some folks did the shooting, and other folks did the dying. Some folks get to tell their side of things, and other folks don't. Some of that depends on what folks think a man is capable of—you know, are men generally good, or are men generally bad?

Well, that's getting a little philosophical, Mr. Redeye. We're not really interested in more general questions. We'd just like to know what you think about one man, one particular man.

Why is it important to you what I think?

Well, we want to know what kind of man Tad Montgomery, or Thaddeus Roe, was. That issue kind of reflects on how we interpret a lot of different events. We can talk about the facts of August 25 all we want, and the facts of August 22nd. And we've done a good bit of that already. But facts don't necessarily tell the whole truth.

What kind of man was Mr. Roe? Was he the hero of Avery? Or was he the desperado called Three Card Monte? Because what happened in Libby seems to support the latter view.

Does it? Does it, now? Well, look. That's a pretty complicated question you're asking me, ain't it?

Look here, just how much longer is this going to go on? I'm getting mighty hungry. If you get my meaning.

MR. MERCKX: Off the record.

(Discussion ensued off the record.)

(A recess was taken from 4:15 p.m. until 4:35 p.m.)

MR. SLAUGHTER: It's 4:30 p.m.

MR. MERCKX: I would like to put on the record that I was carefully calculating the time that Mr. Redeye was under oath today and it was five hours and twenty minutes.

MR. SLAUGHTER: Let the record reflect that we started at 11:00 o'clock and went until 4:00. Okay.

MR. MERCKX: Thank you.

Does this mean I can eat now?

(Deposition adjourned at 4:40 p.m.)

CERTIFICATE
STATE OF IDAHO

I hereby certify that the foregoing transcript was reported, as stated in the caption, and that the questions and answers thereto were reduced to typewriting under my direction; that the foregoing pages 1 through 112 represent a true, complete, and correct transcript of the evidence given upon said hearing, and I further certify that I am not of kin or counsel to the parties in the case; am not in the employ of counsel for any of said parties; nor am I anywise interested in the result of said case.

This, the 18th day of January, 1911.

PHYLLIS M. BEDYNEK

EPILOGUE

Whether the gray of the smoke and ash that had blown the streets of Libby for the previous five days was darker than the rat's nest atop the head of the crone at Billy Blew's was a tough call. But it didn't matter. The smoke still wandered the deserted streets and hid the morning sun, and Dunn Creek Nell still haunted the worn floorboards and the tarnished brass rails at Blew's.

Back in '92, though, Libby had been a smaller town, and a wilder. The glad-handing flow of filthy lucre that habitually accompanied gold and silver mines across the frontier found its way up and down the Kootenai that year, and the easy prosperity brought with it the usual surplus of saloons, claim jumpers, dance hall girls, sure thing artists, lawlessness and outlaws.

Billy Blew's was a saloon at the head of Mineral Avenue. The Idaho mining strikes of '92 had been bitter, and that summer Blew's place saw the end of one of the strike's uglier aftershocks. As with the bombing that later killed Idaho's Governor Steunenberg, no one really knew for sure who was responsible for killing Wild Bill "Ash" Montgomery's wife: but it has always been assumed it was someone linked to the union; or, more properly, someone linked to an intense dislike for Wild Bill. And so he came to Libby that Wednesday, and to Billy Blew's, looking for trouble and a man named Thomas Fewkes. He found both.

Dunn Creek Nell was at the bar that day in 1892, and as she looked through the window of Blew's Saloon down the shank of the T from the head of Mineral Avenue, she saw Bill Montgomery coming up the hardpack from the Libby ferry. Dunn Creek Nell wasn't the only one who saw him coming, but she may have been the only one who really saw what happened when Wild Bill Montgomery died. All the county paper would later offer was, "One day he ran into the wrong man with a .44 Smith and Wesson and was removed from things earthly."

On Thursday morning, August 25th, 1910, Blew's was no longer a saloon. In truth, it was no longer even Blew's. But it still fronted Mineral Avenue, and Dunn Creek Nell still haunted its worn floorboards and tarnished brass rails. And so it was that Dunn Creek Nell was the first to see through the smoke and ash of the Big Blowup of 1910 that Three Card Monte had come to town, walking up Mineral Avenue from the Libby Ferry in search of Blew's—and a man named Thomas Fewkes.

"Damn," she said as she laid down her fork. "Damn if he don't walk like his daddy."

Epilogue

The deposition of John William Redeye was discovered behind wallboards of the old Troy courthouse when it was remodeled in 1986.

The uncredited article from the Seattle *Sunday Times*, dated August 28, 1910, is reprinted in its entirety.

The letter from Tad Montgomery, AKA Thaddeus Roe, to an undisclosed recipient was found in the possession of Roxanne (Fewkes) DeBuse when she died in Yakima, Washington, in 1997, at the age of one hundred and fifteen.

www.ingramcontent.com/pod-product-compliance
Lightning Source LLC
Chambersburg PA
CBHW020611310726
48979CB00008B/1439/J
9780978755454